I0593929

DEADLINES & DRYADS

A TERRA HAVEN CHRONICLES PREQUEL

REBECCA CHASTAIN

This book is a work of fiction. Names, characters, dialogue, places, and incidents either are drawn from the author's imagination or are used fictitiously. Any resemblance to actual persons, living or dead, business establishments, locales, or events is entirely coincidental.

Copyright © 2017 by Rebecca Chastain
Excerpt *A Fistful of Evil* copyright © by Rebecca Chastain
Cover design by Yocla Designs
www.rebeccachastain.com

All rights reserved. In accordance with the US Copyright Act of 1976, scanning, uploading, and electronic sharing of any part of this book without permission of the author constitute unlawful piracy and theft of the author's intellectual property. No part of this book may be used or reproduced in any manner whatsoever without written permission, except in the case of brief quotations embodied in critical articles and reviews. If you would like to use material from this book (other than for review purposes), prior written permission must be obtained from the publisher. Please do not participate in or encourage piracy of copyrighted materials in violation of the author's rights.

Mind Your Muse Books
PO Box 374
Rocklin, CA 95677

ISBN: 978-0-9992385-5-4

ALSO BY REBECCA CHASTAIN

NOVELS OF TERRA HAVEN

GARGOYLE GUARDIAN CHRONICLES

Magic of the Gargoyles

Curse of the Gargoyles

Secret of the Gargoyles

Lured (a novelette)

TERRA HAVEN CHRONICLES

Deadlines & Dryads (prequel)

Leads & Lynxes (forthcoming)

THE MADISON FOX ADVENTURES

A Fistful of Evil

A Fistful of Fire

A Fistful of Frost (forthcoming)

STAND ALONE

Tiny Glitches

NEVER MISS ANY NOVEL NEWS:

Join Rebecca's newsletter to receive emails regarding future releases, bonus content, and behind-the-scenes information.

Visit RebeccaChastain.com

For Cody, always

ACKNOWLEDGMENTS

Though I always planned on writing a trilogy for Kylie, *Deadlines and Dryads* was an unexpected bonus—and such a fun one for me! I love getting to write in this universe, and as always, I'm incredibly grateful to you for reading my novels and making this dream possible.

I'm lucky to have a wonderful team of people backing me. For starters, I have the best beta readers! Thank you to Amy Nguyen, Sarah Gibson, Barbara Hamm, Sara Ehrlich, Liz Perez, Renea Hoff, and Will Looij for pointing out pacing problems and character inconsistencies that I missed in my edits.

To my powerhouse editing team, Carrie Andrews and Amanda Zeier, thank you for catching all the mistakes my eyes passed right over; this book is so much more shiny because of you two!

Thank you to my mom, Teri Chastain, for naming the dryads' grove. Now I can't imagine it as anything other than Emerald Crown Grove.

Will Looij, thank you for giving the gryphon rider her

name. The moment I saw your suggestion, I knew Raquel was the perfect fit.

Of course, thank you, Cody, for you unflagging faith and support. I couldn't do this without you—nor would I want to.

Constructive Elements

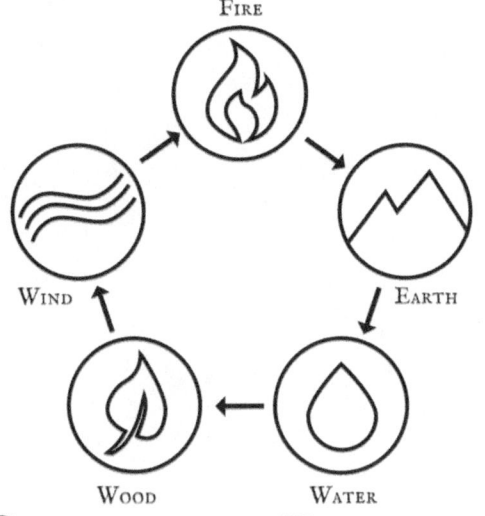

Destructive Elements

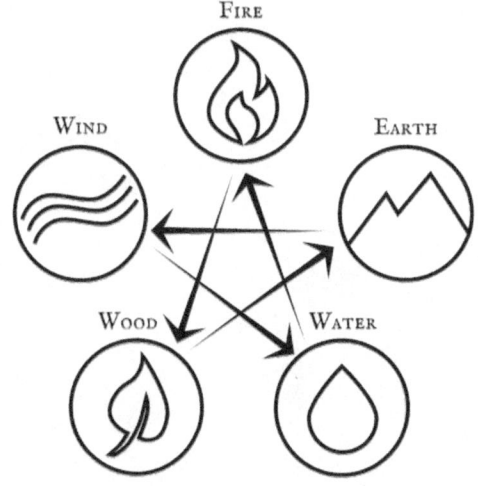

I drummed my fingers on my open notebook, resisting the urge to bounce in my seat. Tension crackled in the charged air of the writers' bullpen, where every single *Terra Haven Chronicle* reporter had gathered this morning at the behest of the editor in chief. She'd given no reason for the meeting, and speculations buzzed through the curiosity-saturated atmosphere.

"Does this happen often?" I asked the junior journalist next to me, who had been at the paper a few months longer than me. I had to raise my voice to be heard above the energized hubbub.

"No. Whatever's going on, it's big."

The editor's door cracked open, and all conversations in the room died off. Everyone leaned forward when Raquel Jervier, the newspaper's gryphon scout, sauntered out. She swept her gaze over our rapt faces and grinned, her white teeth bright against her dark face. Unperturbed by everyone's intense scrutiny, she took a seat at an empty desk, leaning the chair back on two legs to prop her heavy boots on the desk's corner. The writer nearest her started to whisper a question but immediately quieted when Dahlia Bearpaw, the editor in chief, strode into the bullpen, coffee cup in hand. With short, spiky gray hair and a wiry, regal bearing, Dahlia looked as much a gryphon rider as Raquel —and had been in her youth. Now she ran the paper with the same firm hand.

"I think I might have a riot in here if I don't get right to the point," Dahlia said, taking in our eager expressions. "So, here's the deal: The western everlasting tree is starting to bud."

A collective exclamation of excitement exploded across the room, but I remained frozen in place, my thoughts pinging so fast that I temporarily forgot how to move. Forty years ago, one of the immortal trees in Asia had bloomed. It had been the first everlasting tree to show signs of fertility in centuries, and people had flocked to it. Standing beneath its blooming branches, they had asked their myriad questions. In response, the tree had unleashed a flurry of seeds, one per person, no two seeds alike. Just as legend had foretold, the seeds had served as maps of sorts, guiding each person to their answers—if they put in the time and due diligence. It hadn't mattered the nature of their inquiries—personal or professional, selfish or altruistic; the tree had answered them all.

Everlasting trees were as rare as their bloomings; fewer than two existed per continent, and each released its seeds once every century, if not once every half millennium. I never thought an everlasting tree would bloom in my lifetime, especially not the tree nearest Terra Haven.

"Calm down. I know it's exciting, but I haven't finished my announcement," Dahlia shouted above the uproar. "The *Chronicle* is going to send two journalists." Silence dropped over the room as every writer leaned in, waiting to hear who she would select. "The lead journalist on the story will be Audrey Cintrón, but I have yet to pick who will accompany her."

A sea of envious gazes swept to Audrey, who exchanged a solemn nod with the editor. A veteran journalist with decades of experience at the *Chronicle*, Audrey had earned her right to attend this monumental event. Her elegant, precise prose made her the perfect choice, and I strove to rein in my jealousy. From my table at the back of the room, cramped elbow to elbow with the other first-year journalists, I studied the remaining senior writers with a bitter eye. This was a story of a lifetime, and it had come years too early for me.

I mentally tabulated my savings, my connections, and my current standing at the paper. I didn't have the finances to reach the everlasting tree on my own, and I didn't know anybody with the resources to get me there, either. Even if I did, I couldn't afford to take the weeks off work the trip would necessitate, not if I expected to have my job waiting for me when I got home. A knot of resentment settled in my gut, and I leaned back in my chair, defeated.

"Before you all bombard me with your qualifications—which I already know, or you wouldn't be here," Dahlia continued, "let me deliver the next announcement: The position for the second journalist will be determined by whoever brings me the best story in the next forty-eight hours."

I shot from my chair so fast it tumbled over backward. I had a chance!

The room around me had erupted in similar reactions, though several senior writers looked less than pleased. I couldn't muster any sympathy for them. I had written a few good articles for the paper, which was why I had a seat in this room, but I was far from one of the editors' go-to writers when it came to handing out assignments. If I could win this competition, not only would it prove to Dahlia that I had what it took to cover the everlasting tree, but it would also cement my career at the *Chronicle*.

Dahlia's astute gaze cataloged everyone's reactions, including mine as I sheepishly straightened my chair. When she called for silence again, everyone was quick to comply.

"You may have noticed Hernando isn't here today. I sent him out before dawn to cover an invasion of poisonous serpents spotted in Lincoln River, upstream of the city. You'll need to top that story to have a shot at winning."

A collective groan filled the room. Lincoln River flowed straight through Terra Haven and served as the primary source of drinking water for a greater portion of the city. The deadly serpents would be a huge story for the *Chronicle*, and one not easily topped.

My hand shot into the air, and I waved it around to get the editor's attention, but she was already pivoting in my direction.

"Unsurprisingly, the first question comes from junior journalist Kylie Grayson," Dahlia said, her tone wry.

"She's always got the most questions because she doesn't have a clue what she's doing," Nathan said, pitching his voice to carry across the room from his corner desk in the senior writers' section.

I ignored him. I wouldn't let him shame my curiosity. "When will the chosen journalists leave?" I asked.

"As soon as I've made my selection," Dahlia said. "Even traveling gryphonback, the trip will take you several days, and we can't predict when the everlasting tree will release its seeds. I want reporters on the ground posthaste. This is a once-in-a-generation story that deserves more than a few articles; I want to run a special edition, perhaps a series of special editions."

I hadn't thought the room could get any more tense, but at the potent words *special edition*, every single writer went on point. A special edition would mean dozens of articles. Split between only two journalists, we'd each get entire spreads to fill. Contemplating all that column space left me light-headed with yearning.

"One last thing," Dahlia said. "If you've got the vacation time and you'd rather attend the blooming at your own expense, I'll accept the first five vacation requests."

Half the room surged toward the editor, and in the chaos, I slipped out the back. I didn't have the vacation time to use even if I did have the money to get halfway across the country in a few days.

I passed through the exit into the sunlight and paused, realizing I didn't know where to go. I had a few rumor scouts in the field, and I had a few leads I could follow up on, but would any of them evolve into a story spectacular enough to win me this competition?

I pulled my journal out of my bag and opened it to peruse my notes, moving to the edge of the sidewalk to get out of the way of foot traffic. The city had woken up while I'd been inside, and the downtown streets bustled with people headed to their jobs. A horse-drawn wagon trundled past, the driver fighting the reins as the team shied at the sight of the enormous gryphon perched atop the *Chronicle*'s two-story roof. I tilted my head back and acknowledged the tiny shiver of fear that darted down my spine when the gryphon cocked her massive eagle head and pinned me with a golden eye. Rationally, I knew she was Raquel's tame companion and would never eat a human, but my instincts still kicked in, telling me to run. Suppressing them, I scanned the rest of the roofline for Quinn's bright citrine face, but when I didn't spot the gargoyle, I turned back to my notebook.

The door burst open beside me, and Nathan stepped out, sweeping his dark hair off his forehead in a practiced motion. Lanky, with a perpetual black, bristly beard and thick-framed glasses, he looked like a caricature of a hard-working investigative reporter—a style he'd obviously culti-vated. He spotted me and grinned, spinning on a toe to confront me.

"Tell me that was for show," he said. "You don't *actually* believe you can snag a story that's more impressive than anything a senior writer can get, do you?"

"You heard Dahlia. We all have a shot."

"Come on, Kylie. You've been here less than six months. You don't have a chance."

"I've had two front-page stories already," I said, knowing I shouldn't let him goad me but unable to help myself. "How many front-page stories have you had in that time?"

Nathan's thin lips tightened and he shoved his hands into his pockets. Score one for me.

"You got lucky. Twice," he said. "But this time you can't just wait around for an article to fall into your lap. Or do you plan to pump your gargoyle friend for another story?"

I pushed my hair out of my face and gave him my best glare. I hated that he was partially right; I had been lucky in landing two major stories before anybody else knew they were happening, thanks to my best friend, Mika. In the last couple months, she had rescued several gargoyles and had become the city's one and only gargoyle healer. The very first story that had gotten me noticed by Dahlia had been the tale of Mika's daring rescue of the gargoyles. A small part of me wished I were bringing that story to the editor now, because it would have guaranteed me a victory in this competition. Now I needed to present Dahlia with something even more impressive, and every lead in my notebook fell well short.

Not that I would admit as much to Nathan.

"Don't worry about me," I said, injecting false sweetness into my voice. "I already have another amazing story lined up."

"You do? Just like that?"

"I do." I managed to infuse confidence I didn't feel into those two words.

Tilting my journal so Nathan couldn't see its contents, I scanned my notes again. Maybe the thefts at the fish market would develop into something bigger than petty crime. If not, I might be able to spin the story into a larger commentary addressing the socioeconomic disparities . . . Ugh. No. Maybe I *would* have to hunt down Mika and see if she had encountered any new gargoyles in trouble. Of course, Dahlia might not be impressed with a third story in a row about gargoyles.

"You're riding high on your past successes, but don't let your beginner's luck fool you," Nathan cautioned, his patronizing tone setting my teeth on edge. "Do yourself a favor and don't burn yourself out trying to compete with experienced journalists. Put in the time, put in the legwork, and you'll eventually pull in some big stories on your own."

This wasn't the first time Nathan had given me his "sage advice," which basically amounted to *take it slow* and *don't upstage senior writers*. I had no intention of listening to him. "I'm not sure why you're concerned about what I'm going to write if you're so certain your story will be superior."

"Oh, I'm not worried. It's just I see promise in you, and I

don't want you to get your spirit crushed before you even start your career."

Two front-page stories! I wanted to shout. My career had already started, and it'd begun with a bang.

"I'm flattered you noticed my journalistic skills. Excuse me, Nathan, I've got to run." I snapped my journal shut and stalked off before he could say anything else—or before I said something I'd regret.

I hadn't made it halfway down the block when I spotted my rumor scout barreling down on me. The snarl of elemental energy whipped through the air, tight bands of air and fire woven through thinner strands of earth, water, and wood, all of it holding precious information. I glanced back over my shoulder and picked up my pace. Nathan tracked my retreat, and his eyes narrowed when he caught sight of my elemental creation. Damn it.

Half jogging, I met the rumor scout at the end of the block. Shaped from my magic, it honed in on me with a precision that had taken years to perfect. I shoved my hair out of the way as the bundle of magic coiled over my right ear, forming a soundproof seal against my scalp. Immediately, a stranger's voice spoke into my ear, the words having been collected and recorded by the scout.

". . . dryad chased me. I've never seen anything like it. I've taken Wicker Road hundreds of times, and I've seen my share of dryads, but not like this." The man's deep voice held the accent of a Southern merchant, and he sounded out of breath. He didn't pause to give whoever he was talking to a chance to speak, either. "The dryads looked . . . looked . . . predatory."

Predatory? Dryads were peaceful creatures. They lived in harmony with the trees to which their lives were bonded, and their personalities were the equivalent of an oak given mobility. They nurtured the forest and they lived quiet, hidden lives. I couldn't even picture what a predatory dryad would look like; it was like trying to picture a hostile tree—one that had apparently chased this man.

My journalistic instincts perked up.

I had been hearing rumors about increased restlessness in the local Emerald Crown Grove dryads since the tail end of winter, which was why I'd tailored a rumor scout to seek out and record any conversations in which the word *dryad* was mentioned. I'd also read up on dryads at the city library, learning that their abnormal agitation could be due to an impending violent storm or a possible encroachment of a new road or predator into their grove. I'd held off pitching the story to Dahlia because I had my own, third theory that involved the timing of the dryads' restlessness, but I'd been waiting for it to pan out.

I hadn't even considered that the dryad story might be worthy of today's challenge, but this new development held promise. Maybe I wouldn't need to go to the fish market after all.

"Don't do it," the anxious voice continued. "You don't want to chance—"

Claws of air magic ripped the rumor scout from my ear, tearing out a hunk of my hair.

"Ow!"

I spun around. Nathan clutched my rumor scout in a thick lasso of air and held it suspended in front of him, studying it with avid curiosity.

Double damn.

2

"Hey! That's mine." Rubbing my stinging scalp, I stalked back to Nathan and lashed a sharp blade of earth magic at his lasso trap. He effortlessly evaded my strike. I planted my hands on my hips, readying another knife of earth. "Give it back."

"This looks like a communication capsule, but you've done something different with the knots of fire," Nathan said. He pushed it against his ear, but when nothing happened, he went back to twisting the rumor scout in the air in front of him, inspecting it from every angle.

I made another futile attempt to cut through his magic, my hands balling into fists when I failed.

He was right; the rumor scout closely resembled a normal communication capsule, but I'd made a number of modifications and, through painstaking experimentation, had figured out how to combine the recording properties of a communication capsule with the honing properties of a finder's spell. I'd also fine-tuned the weaves to release their captured sounds only to me, just in case they were intercepted. To my knowledge, no one else had ever created anything similar. Rumor scouts were my secret weapon, and even if Nathan would never be able to crack open the contents of this particular rumor scout, I wasn't about to let him rip off my design.

"Is that an inverted knot?" Nathan pulled the scout in for a closer inspection.

With a silent curse, I reshaped my elemental weapon into a combination of earth and water, and jabbed it straight through the rumor scout. The fragile spell imploded, the elements dispersing, releasing the recorded words in an unintelligible rush. I'd lost whatever information had remained inside its weaves, but keeping the knowledge of how to build a rumor scout from Nathan took precedence. Besides, I'd heard enough.

"Where did you learn how to do that?" Nathan demanded.

"None of your business." I spun on my heel and stormed down the street.

Nathan dogged my steps. "If you're withholding tools that could benefit the *Chronicle*, I'll tell Dahlia."

"You do that." I veered down a side street, hoping to shake him, but Nathan followed.

"Where are you off to in such a hurry?"

"Away from you. I thought that was obvious."

"That's funny, I figured you just received some important information. Maybe something worthy of a newspaper article."

"Hardly," I snapped, but I knew my anger wouldn't fool him. He might be annoying, but he had a journalist's nose for a story.

Magic blossomed inside me, my natural capacity for the

elements doubling between one step and the next. I tripped, then steadied, looking around for Quinn. All gargoyles had the ability to enhance magic in others, but Quinn was the only gargoyle who made a point of always boosting my magic when he was within range. I treasured the privilege as much as I did his trust and friendship.

A golden-winged lion surged over the roofline to my left. With the early-morning rays glistening on the underside of his wings, he looked as if he were sculpted from the sun itself, and my breath caught at the beauty of him. Then Quinn tucked his wings and plummeted into the shadowed alley. At the last possible second, he slowed his descent and landed with an explosive clap of quartz paws against cobble-stones, clattering a few steps as his momentum carried him forward.

I shielded my eyes from a flurry of dust raised by his landing and backed up to give him room. Despite being nearly the size of an adult lion, the young gargoyle hadn't finished growing, and his coordination occasionally suffered. Today, excitement made him prance in place.

"Kylie! I've got information about our FPD squad!" Quinn announced, his voice deep and his words lisping slightly around his long canines.

A thrill went through me. *Our* FPD squad could only mean the band of five elite full-spectrum Federal Pentagon Defense warriors led by Captain Grant Monaghan. Anything he was involved in was worth pursuing—because Grant's squad defended Terra Haven from extreme, story-worthy dangers, not because the captain happened to be blessed with rugged good looks and a muscular body to match—but I clamped down on my questions, intensely aware of Nathan's curiosity beside me.

"I didn't know you had the gargoyle doing your scout work," Nathan said.

I turned my back to him, trying to discreetly signal Quinn to silence. "That's great, Quinn, but I'm sure it can wait—"

"It can't wait! The FPD got called to Emerald Crown Grove. I heard it from my friend at the city guard station. Whatever's going on in the grove, it's bigger than we thought."

"They call in the FPD for pretty much anything these days," I said, making another shushing gesture at Quinn. "It's probably nothing."

The gargoyle wrinkled his expressive brows at me. "But you told me to always tell you whenever I heard anything about the FPD, especially Gra—"

"I think this can wait," I interrupted in a rush.

"If Kylie doesn't want to hear," Nathan said, "why don't you tell me?"

The naïve gargoyle glanced back and forth between us, shifting nervously on his thick paws, his expression twisted in confusion. Any other day, I would have already been running toward the action, bombarding him for information on the way.

"What's happening in Emerald Crown Grove?" Nathan prompted.

I gritted my teeth. I could ill afford to lose this juicy story to the senior writer, not with the everlasting tree competition on the line, but I was forced to admit it was too late to keep this lead to myself. My dismissal of the city's most elite warriors hadn't fooled anyone, especially not the senior writer. We both knew everything the FPD did was newspaper worthy. Even if Quinn said nothing more, Nathan was sure to investigate the grove.

"Go ahead," I said.

"The FPD is turning people away from the grove, and they're not allowing travel through any part of the forest." Quinn delivered the last of his shocking news in a subdued tone.

"What's the threat?" Nathan asked.

"I don't know."

"How many FPD were called?"

"I don't know."

"Did you get anything else?" Nathan had the audacity to sound exasperated.

Quinn shook his head, his wide mouth drawn down. He cast a woeful glance in my direction, and I tried to give him a reassuring smile, but it was difficult with my teeth fused together in frustration.

"Good, good. If you hear anything else, be sure to report to me. You, too, Kylie." Nathan gave me a smug smile. "As a senior writer, I have plenty of experience investigating dangerous events like these." He sauntered back toward the *Chronicle*, his steps a smidgen too fast to be casual. I wouldn't put it past him to start running the moment he slipped out of sight. I glowered after him until he turned the corner.

"Who does he think he is?" I fumed. "This is my story! I found it. I put my scouts on it. I asked you to keep an ear out for news about the FPD. And now Nathan acts like I haven't worked with the FPD before on hazardous stories. I covered the black market exposé! I covered Focal Park." I paced back and forth, pounding my fists against my thighs as I ranted.

"Did I do something wrong?"

I took in Quinn's anxious expression and rushed to his side, crouching to his eye level. "No, I'm not mad at you.

Nathan is the low-down scumbag story thief. You are wonderful."

"Does that mean you're happy with the information I found?"

"You bet!" I ran my hand down his side, the grooves of his stone scales soft beneath my fingertips. Of all the gargoyles Mika had rescued, I secretly believed Quinn to be the prettiest. Not only did he have an amber-gold lion body of solid citrine, but also his falcon wings were well proportioned and magnificent, each stone feather a marvel of meticulous detail. Behind the wavy lines of his stone ruff, dragon scales dressed him from his shoulders to his tail, and oversized paws hinted at growth still to come; when he reached his full size, he would be big enough to ride.

Quinn leaned subtly into my touch, and his smile widened far enough to flash his canines.

"Are we going to investigate?" he asked.

"Of course! And we're going to beat Nathan, too. Come on."

———

I EMPTIED MY WALLET INTO THE HANDS OF THE PROPRIETOR OF Jolene's Speedy Rugs, receiving in return a scrap of carpet hardly bigger than a throw pillow.

"This is the largest you've got?" I asked.

Jolene held up my money. "This is the largest you can afford."

I sighed and settled into a cramped cross-legged position atop the rented rug. Jolene activated its flying spell, and the carpet lifted me two feet off the ground. A subtle net of air folded around my legs, holding me to the flimsy surface.

"You have the rug for half an hour. You steer by

adjusting the rudder like so," she said, demonstrating by turning the wooden handle at the front of the rug. The rudder shifted beneath me, the vibration discernible through the thin fabric.

"Yes, I know. This isn't my first time on a flying carpet."

"You stop by deactivating the thrusters," she continued as if I hadn't spoken, pointing to the complex cones of air element attached to the back corners of the rug. "The rug is to remain outdoors at all times. If you attempt to take it inside, the homing spell will activate and it will return to me. If you attempt to modify the rug, it will return to me. If you attempt to detain it after your session ends, you will be responsible for all personal injury or property damaged when it returns to me. Anything you break while on the rug is your responsibility."

When she finally freed me to leave, I shot through the bay door of her shop and pointed the carpet southeast, toward Wicker Road and Emerald Crown Grove. My blond hair streamed out behind me, and the hem of my cotton shirt fluttered at my waistband. Impatience slithered beneath my skin. The rug was faster than running and faster than the bus, but it wasn't fast enough. In my head, Nathan raced ahead of me on a sleek personal flying carpet, slipping inside a last-minute containment ward just before it crashed closed. While he cozied up to Captain Grant Monaghan's squad, I'd be barricaded outside, waiting to read the details in tomorrow's paper.

Using a subtle probe of fire-laced air, I tested the thrusters to see if I could coax more speed from them, but the lock on their spell thwarted me.

I kept an eye on the sky, tracking Quinn's progress above me. He could fly a lot faster than the rug, so he scouted ahead and directed me down side streets and alleys to avoid any slowdowns. We made great time through downtown Terra Haven, then along the warehouse district on the southeast side. When I hit Wicker Road, I leaned forward on the carpet, trying to use aerodynamics to my advantage. The last buildings in the city zipped by on either side, giving way to the oak-studded grove where it abutted the city.

The carpet slammed to a stop against an invisible barrier. My teeth snapped together as I whiplashed forward, arms flying out to catch myself, but the rug's built-in safety spell anchored me atop the tiny surface. My bag flew forward, cutting into the back of my neck and armpit, before dumping its contents onto the dirt road. Fortunately, no one else was on the road, or I might have been run over.

Wheezing, I straightened. The rug had stopped at the exact edge of Terra Haven. Despite having at least five more minutes on the rental, I wouldn't be taking it outside the city. Somehow in her litany of rug rules and regulations, Jolene had failed to mention the most important restriction.

Cursing under my breath, I deactivated the safety spell with a flick of air. The rug dropped to the ground, landing atop my journal. I crawled to my feet. The moment I was free of the rug, it lifted ten feet in the air and zoomed back into the city.

"Is it just me, or is that rug flying twice as fast as before?" I asked Quinn when he landed beside me.

"Maybe it can go faster without a passenger."

"Seems like a stupid design to me." I collected my scattered belongings, brushing them off and stuffing them back in my bag, then turned to face the grove. "Let's go."

A fiery buzz of warning sizzled through my body as I stepped across the invisible boundary between Terra Haven and the forest. I shook off the clinging weaves, sluicing my body and Quinn's with water magic. The FPD couldn't encircle the entirety of Emerald Crown Grove with a ward, so they'd done the next-best thing: place warning beacons at the main thoroughfare. Disregarding the warning wasn't illegal, but some might consider it foolish. I considered it my journalistic duty and proceeded into the forest without pause.

It had been a few years since I had traveled this road, and I'd forgotten how quickly the city disappeared. Dense woods and the rolling hills blocked out Terra Haven's skyline after the first two turns in the road. I wanted to run, but since I didn't know how far we had to go, I settled on a brisk walk I could sustain for hours. Quinn half trotted at my side, moving with the liquid grace of a big cat, his rock paws making less noise than my boots. The midmorning sun slanted through the trees, heating the packed dirt beneath my feet and warming my scalp. A silent wind stirred the branches of the tall oaks on either side of the road, but not even a whisper of moving air reached ground level, and I fanned the front of my shirt to cool myself.

We'd been walking twenty minutes before I realized an unnatural silence cloaked the forest beneath the susurrus of the wind through the oak canopies. No birds sang, no crickets chirped, no small creatures stirred the underbrush or rustled through the dead leaves of the forest floor. I slowed, quieting my footsteps and straining to listen for the missing noises.

"What is it?" Quinn asked.

"It's too quiet. I received a rumor scout before we met up, and the voice in it said he'd been chased from the grove, but there's nothing—"

A pair of coyotes burst from the bushes ahead of us, lips snarled to reveal white canines, ears flat against their skulls. I froze for half a heartbeat, then hunkered next to Quinn's side, drawing a hasty ward of air around us. The coyotes barely registered our presence, veering wide to gallop around us down the opposite side of the road toward Terra Haven. Quinn didn't have time to do more than arch his wings before they raced out of sight around the bend in the road.

"Since when do coyotes use roads?" Quinn asked.

I rubbed my thumb against my tingling fingertips. "Come on; let's find out what's got them spoo—"

A huge buck crashed down the hill to our right, his slender legs springing over smaller bushes. His antlers caught in a low-hanging branch, and he ripped free with a snort, not slowing until he stumbled onto the road. A trio of does bounded after him, their sweat-slicked sides heaving. None gave us a second glance as they raced after the coyotes.

I spun to peer in the direction they'd come from, my curiosity pounding in time with my racing heart. When nothing else emerged, I cautiously dropped my ward.

"I don't think that's a normal wind," Quinn said, studying the foliage twisting above us.

This early in spring, the leaves were bright green and not yet fully developed, but they were large enough to catch air currents and tug the branches. Only, no pattern connected the shifting limbs of one tree and the next, almost as if—

"I don't think that's the wind at all," I whispered. The trees moved, but they did so of their own volition.

We hustled into motion, and I chaffed goose bumps from my arms, eyes trained on the branches' abnormal gyrations. It wasn't my imagination: The oaks grew more active as we approached, their gnarled limbs straining toward us. By unspoken consent, we shifted to the middle of the narrow road as we strove to detect other noises above the creaks and groans of the trees. I tore my gaze from the canopies, searching the forest around us for an explanation. Trees didn't animate themselves, not even those bound to dryads. Were the dryads behind this? Was this what the merchant had meant when he said they chased him from Emerald Crown Grove?

"How much farther do you think—"

A narrow hay wagon pulled by a team of oxen thundered out of control around the corner, cutting off my words. They barreled down on us too fast and cumbersome to swerve. Heart in my throat, I threw myself into the weeds at the side of the road. Quinn leapt over me, crashing through a dense manzanita bush. The ground shook beneath the oxen's pounding feet, and I rolled, smashing up against the base of the manzanita and curling tight. From my prone position, I caught a glimpse of the driver clinging to her wooden perch with both hands.

"Not safe! Turn around!" she shouted; then she and her team careened out of sight, and the chaotic drumbeat of the oxen's heavy hooves became submerged beneath the increasingly loud soughs of the giant oaks around us.

I picked myself up, tugging my shirt over my nose to filter out the billowing dust while I brushed dirt and weeds from my clothes and prevailed upon my fluttering heart to migrate from my throat back to my chest. Quinn shook free of the shattered remains of the manzanita and crept to the edge of the road.

I studied both directions of Wicker Road, convincing myself that my taut nerves had everything to do with anticipation of an exciting story and narrowly avoiding being trampled and nothing to do with fear.

Something ran a claw up my back and I screamed and

dashed to the center of the road before spinning to confront my attacker. The long limb of an oak sprang back to its natural position, the twig tips writhing as if frustrated to have had me slip through their grasps. I shuddered but forced myself to keep walking deeper into the forest. If Nathan was ahead of me, I needed to catch up, and if he was behind me, I didn't want to waste time and *let* him catch up.

Sure, that's why I had to contain the impulse to bolt at every sharp squeak and ominous groan.

"Do you think we should go back?" Quinn asked. He shrank in on himself as he crept beside me, his belly inches from touching the ground, his small, round ears flat against his skull.

Guilt pierced my heart. I was getting a story out of this, but Quinn was here only to support me. I shouldn't be dragging him into danger.

"I need to keep going, but it would really help me if you were in the air." He wouldn't return to Terra Haven if I asked him to, which made getting him above the trees' reach the best option. He would be safe and I would still be able to use his magical enhancement if I needed the boost. The rationalization sounded mercenary and cold, and I opened my mouth to urge Quinn back to Terra Haven but stopped myself for the same reason as before. Quinn had come with me because we were friends. He'd no sooner abandon me than I would him, and I wouldn't insult him by asking him to go. "Stay up there, and if you see anything bad happen to me, go for help."

"Are you sure?"

"I'm sure." I patted his shoulder, trying to look reassuring. Tension thrummed my nerves, but I couldn't bring myself to turn around. My journalistic instincts urged me forward. Whatever had riled this forest, it was important.

The story was too big to turn my back on, especially not with the chance to go to the everlasting tree on the line.

"Okay. I'll stick close."

Quinn trotted ahead of me a few steps, then spread his stone wings wide and launched into the sky. He climbed almost straight up, twisting aside when thick oak branches clutched at him. I didn't breathe until he cleared the canopy.

Then I turned and faced the seething forest alone.

3

I broke into a jog, telling myself I was hurrying to catch up with Nathan. If my heart hadn't been knocking against my chest like I'd already run a mile, I might have believed myself. Prickles ran down my spine, and I jerked to check behind me. The road remained empty, but the sight didn't reassure me. Giant oaks on either side of the road twisted and scraped against each other, their branches moaning and cracking as they flexed. The noise level rose and fell in an unintelligible language, but the message came through loud and clear: *Danger. Run away.*

I kept my steps measured, knowing that if I gave in to the compulsion to sprint, I wouldn't be able to slow again until my legs gave out.

"Come on, FPD squad. Where are you?"

At the sound of my voice, the nearest trees convulsed, long branches thrashing across the road, clawing for me. I shied, and the tree on the opposite side scratched a limb into the strap of my bag, tangling a cluster of slender twigs around my bicep. Clamping down on a scream, I yanked free, tucked my bag under one arm, and bolted. The oaks raged, roiling in a furor as I tore past them, their collective noises blending into a chilling many-throated moan. In the periphery of my vision, their writhing bodies transformed into monsters, and I whipped my head back and forth, striving vainly to keep the entire grove in sight. When I tripped, I caught myself with a hand planted in the sharp gravel and surged back to my feet, gulping air.

Flashes of Quinn's golden shape flickered above me, and the sight of him calmed the terrified chatter of my unraveling thoughts. I wasn't alone. Drawing deeply on the magic inside me, I held the raw elements ready.

This story better be spectacular, I thought. My lungs burned and pain lanced my side with every pounding step, but panic rode too close to the surface to allow me to slow.

I pelted around a bend in the road, sprinting into a narrow grassy meadow—right into a trap. A heavy band lashed around my midsection, lifting me, my still-pumping legs churning empty air. Terror clogged my throat and I flailed, every defensive spell evaporating in my panic. I clawed into the restraint constricting around my waist, expecting to encounter the rough bark of an oak. Instead, my fingers slid against slick cables of air strengthened by delicate fibers of wood element.

"Damn it, Kylie! What are you doing here?"

When his words penetrated my frenzy, I froze; then I whipped my head around, peering through snarls of blond hair at Captain Grant Monaghan. Dizzying relief flooded my body, and I sagged against his sturdy magic.

Grant lowered me to the ground and released me. I bent in half, resting my hands against my knees while I caught my breath, my face hidden as I struggled to regain my composure. Around us, the trees seethed, the cracks and snaps of their branches so loud that it drowned out my ragged breathing.

"Are you spying on me again?" Grant demanded.

I swiped sweat from my forehead and didn't look up from my toes. "I see your ego's still twice as large as you, Captain." Which was saying something, given the man's stature. He stood a mere head taller than me, but next to his broad shoulders and muscular frame, I never failed to feel tiny.

"Answer the question: What are you doing here?" He narrowed the distance between us, looming above me.

I straightened, pushing my hair out of my face. Seeing him had eased my full-throttle terror—not that I would ever admit to Grant how scared I had been—and I met his dark gaze with a measure of calm. From his severe haircut, graced with a peppering of gray at the temples, to his broad shoulders held straight and square to his trim waist and thick thighs, Grant gave the impression he could halt a runaway train by sheer willpower and perhaps the use of one bulging bicep.

In other words, he epitomized the image of an FPD captain, and he tended to believe he could boss everyone around, not just the members of his squad.

I rolled my shoulders back, lifted my chin, and countered his question with one of my own. "Where's the rest of your squad?"

"Busy." He surveyed the agitated trees, then pinned me with a hard glare. "You need to take your damn tracker off me."

"I've never had a tracker on you in my life!" I planted my hands on my hips and did my best to look offended. As captain of the preeminent FPD squad in Terra Haven, Grant often operated at the center of the city's most intriguing stories, and I'd made it a habit to have at least three rumor scouts circulating at all times, hunting out instances of his name. But I had never once put a tracker on the man.

Of course, if I could have done so without him spotting my clumsy magic and destroying it, I would have.

"Then what are you doing here?" Grant's square jaw bunched and he looked like he wanted to shake me. "Are you blind as well as foolish? Can't you see something is wrong? I put up a warning beacon for this exact reason: This is no place for a civilian."

"I'm not here as a civilian; I'm here as a reporter and—"

Grant spun and thrust me behind him. A second later I heard pounding hoofbeats. Grant readied another net of air, and I eased sideways to peer around him.

A wild-eyed mare galloped into the clearing, spotted us, and planted her back feet, skidding to a halt on the dirt road. The rider snapped forward and would have flown over the horse's neck if she hadn't reared. Arms flailing, the rider tumbled to the ground. The mare whinnied, spun on a back hoof, and galloped back the way she'd come. Nathan rolled onto his back, groaning.

"Why, Captain, your callous disregard for that man's well-being was shocking," I said, privately pleased Grant had made no effort to break Nathan's fall.

"It was safer not to intervene," Grant said, shooting me a sharp glance.

Nathan picked himself up and dusted himself off. My petty delight soured when I realized that the loss of his horse decreased my odds of being able to get rid of Nathan.

"Who are you?" Grant asked.

Nathan shoved his glasses into place and extended his hand, his eyes lighting up. "Nathan Aspell, sir, senior writer on staff at the *Terra Haven Chronicle*. I recognize you from your noble work. It's an honor to meet you, Captain Monaghan."

Grant shook his hand, casting a dark look in my direction. I glared right back. It wasn't as if I had invited Nathan along.

"Terra Haven is lucky to have such skilled Federal Pentagon Defense warriors as you and your squad defending our streets—and our forests," Nathan continued, his flagrant fawning nauseating me. "Our paper covered everything you did to save Focal Park. I don't know what we would've done if you hadn't been there when the park started to implode."

"Grant hardly did anything," I snapped. It hadn't been "our paper" that had covered the story. It had been me. How convenient of Nathan to overlook that minor detail. "The real hero was the city's gargoyle healer, Mika Stillwater."

Nathan scoffed. "As much as you'd like it, your friend isn't the center of every story."

"Kylie's right; the city owes Mika an enormous debt of gratitude," Grant said.

Nathan's expression pinched at Grant's dismissive tone, and I hid my smile. Tugging the hem of his shirt straight, Nathan cleared his throat.

"Is what's happening here anything like what happened at Focal Park?" he asked, skewing his tone artificially deeper. He'd pulled out his "serious journalist" voice. I decided not to tell him it made him sound asinine.

Grant spared him an incredulous look when he realized Nathan had been serious. "No."

The forest hadn't calmed while we'd talked; if anything, it had grown more frenetic. The captain created a test pentagram of the five elements, each elemental side stretching as long as his arm. He set it spinning around the small meadow. The wood line flared bright, pulsing as if static electricity vibrated along its length. The oaks nearest the pentagram shied back, their branches rubbing together in sharp squeaks and shrieks. Grant collapsed the pentagram.

"You both need to leave. Now. Before you get hurt."

"What's making the trees so active?" I asked. *Active* sounded better than *aggressive* or *scary*.

"Something dangerous, which is why you need to leave."

Nathan fidgeted and glanced back the way his horse had fled, clearly wishing he still had his mount.

"I'm not leaving here until you do," I announced, locking stares with Grant. Sunlight glinted off his eyes, fracturing an amber glow through his dark irises. On Nathan, a day's stubble looked unkempt; on Grant, it only added to his rugged appeal—which I pointedly was not acknowledging, just as I pretended not to notice the shiver that ghosted down my spine when he growled my name.

"Kylie, this is no time to argue."

"Maybe we should listen to him," Nathan said.

I didn't look away from Grant. "You can waste your time trying to kick me out of this public grove, Captain, where I have every right as a citizen of Terra Haven to be." As I predicted, the comment made the muscles in Grant's jaw bunch, and I smiled inwardly. It must be aggravating for him that I didn't jump every time he barked a command. "But I think you have more pressing concerns than arguing with me."

"If you're staying, I'm staying," Nathan said, as if anyone cared.

"So what's the problem?" I asked.

The oaks around the clearing leaned in, interlocking their branches to close the canopy above us. In the deepening gloom, it looked as if the trunks of the trees split open, the bark curling free to reshape into small, humanoid figures no taller than my waist. The dryads stalked forward on wooden limbs that creaked and popped, their twiglike hands clutching sharp wooden spears. Menace defined their movements, and their glossy, ebony gazes promised violence.

Shock locked me in place. By their very nature, dryads were docile and nurturing, not . . . homicidal.

Grant's hand curled around my forearm, yanking me to his side. He snaked his other arm out to drag Nathan close. I spun to look behind us, trepidation growing. Dryads spilled from the forest to enclose us, a circle of sinister wooden spears poised for a deadly assault.

"The problem," Grant said, pitching his voice low, "is the dryads are frenzied."

4

I grabbed every drop of air magic I could hold and prepared a thick air shield, hoping Grant had a plan. Beside me, Nathan cowered against Grant's broad back, eyes darting to take in the maniacal dryads. The closest dryads hissed, the sound reminiscent of twigs scraping a glass pane. My arm hair stood on end, and I flinched when the dryads jabbed the air with their whittled spears. Before I could cast my shield, Grant enveloped us in an impenetrable ward of oak-tuned wood interlaced with a thick layer of air. I altered my grasp of the elements, trying to match Grant's, but I couldn't hold the right ratio of wood to air, and I wasn't adept enough with wood to tune it to the same resonance as oak. My weave unraveled.

A lion's roar split the air, and everyone froze. The limbs above us cracked and snapped as a giant golden boulder plummeted through them, landing with a ground-jarring thud so close to me that I staggered into Grant. Broken twigs and leaves rained down on us, and I shielded my head with an umbrella of solidified air. I drew heavily on the wallop of magic that burst open inside me, grateful to no longer feel so helpless. Quinn reared up on his hind legs and flared his long wings, releasing another ear-ringing roar that made the closest dryads stumble back.

The gargoyle's impressive display warmed my heart as much as his bravery. I shot Grant a pointed look. Even the captain would have to admit the presence of a gargoyle was advantageous, and he had me to thank for that.

Grant stepped around me and bopped Quinn on the nose. "Hush."

The gargoyle dropped to all fours and folded his wings, his shoulders hunching in confusion.

Grant surveyed the dryads, swiveling until he pinpointed a female hanging back near the trees. Like the rest of the dryads, a patchwork of bright green and faded brown leaves camouflaged her trim body, but where most of the dryads possessed gnarled and blackened skin, tones of ash and walnut dappled her bare arms—colors best matched to a young oak. I might have mistaken her for a child or young adult if not for her dark eyes. She studied us with unmistakable maturity and solemnity. Of all the dryads surrounding us, she was the only one not carrying a weapon.

"Potentate Heartwood, you may remember me; I am Grant Monaghan, caretaker of Terra Haven. My companions and I are here to offer aid and protection from whatever threatens this forest."

I frowned. I thought the dryads *were* the threat. If they weren't the reason the forest churned with malicious intent, then what was behind this? And why were they holding us at spear point? I shared a speculative glance with Nathan, then turned away, irritated with myself for acknowledging his presence.

"As proof of my goodwill, I bring you herbal theriaca." Grant opened a small pouch at his waist. From it, he produced an enormous oak leaf wrapped in a delicate preservative weave of water and wood, and at his touch, the fragile living filaments unfurled into a tenuous bowl. Pulling a small glass vile from the pouch, Grant used his teeth to uncork it, then poured the viscous green contents into the leaf. Around us, the dryads leaned forward, eyes intent upon the liquid.

Grant dropped the shield. Quinn edged closer to me, the stone feathers of his wings rustling against each other. I rested a hand on his shoulders, taking comfort from him even as I prepared a new shield to protect us both. Nathan didn't wait, casting a barrier of wood and air around his body so thick it obscured his features. I would have rolled my eyes if I hadn't been tempted to do the same.

But the dryads weren't paying attention to the three of us. All eyes tracked Grant as he stepped forward, holding the enchanted leaf and its contents out to the young dryad leader. Before today, I'd been so certain she lay at the root of the grove's unrest. Instead, she appeared to be the calm force holding the others in check.

The potentate sniffed the air, and the interlocked canopy above us bent inward. Wood magic shimmered, coalescing above our heads into a thick, odorless miasma drawn from deep in the bark of the nearest trees. The formless cloud swept the clearing before funneling into a single tendril that snaked through the air and dipped into Grant's oak leaf. I gaped at the bizarre use of magic, startling when the elemental stem connected with the theriaca and the dryads gasped in unison.

The dryads' magic shattered, millions of wood particulates blasting back to the oaks and disappearing into the rough bark. I'd never seen anything like it.

The army of dryads shuffled, parting to make way for the potentate, and the creaks of their movements emphasized the silence that had fallen over the grove. Grant dropped to one knee, extending his offering. I didn't know enough about dryad culture to know if he did it out of respect or simply to make it easier for the dryad leader to reach the leaf.

Potentate Heartwood hesitated, taking in me and Nathan, her eyes lingering even longer on Quinn. Gargoyles tended to be city creatures, and I wondered if she'd encountered one before. Finally, when absolute silence had fallen over the meadow, she strode forward and took the oak leaf from Grant's hand. He held still as a statue as she dipped her mouth into the leaf and drank. When she lifted her head, a quiver ran through her body, and even in the dim light she looked brighter.

I thought she would speak, but instead she backed up two steps and handed the leaf to the nearest warrior. Then she folded her hands over her stomach and gazed at Grant. He remained on one knee, body relaxed as if he could hold the pose for hours. He seemed equally content to remain in his benign staring match with the potentate, and neither monitored the passage of the herbal theriaca through the dryads.

I relaxed in increments as aggression bled from the legion of dryads. The theriaca must have been a powerful peace offering, and one I planned to learn more about the first moment I could question Grant. In the meantime ...

I sneaked a hand into my bag and pulled out my camera. Using one hand, I unlocked the front and extended the accordion shadowbox and lens, locking them in place with a practiced flick. Normally, I would have lifted the camera to my eye to make the appropriate aperture and focal adjustments, but I didn't want to chance startling the dryads. Holding the camera at my hip, I toggled the aperture wide open to accommodate the shadowy lighting since I didn't dare use the flash, chose the longest shutter speed possible, and attempted to aim through the tiny top-down viewfinder. Holding my breath, I snapped several shots of the potentate, hoping to capture a usable picture. Very few photographs had ever been taken of this quiet and normally shy race.

Shifting marginally, I positioned the potentate and Grant in the same shot. The captain's muscular frame accentuated the delicacy of the dryad, his folded height emphasizing her short stature. A shot of the potentate alone would be a journalistic triumph, but the two of them juxtaposed, the ultimate human warrior kneeling in front of the regal dryad leader, his coiled strength and raw power displayed in an almost vulnerable offering to her, was solid newsstand gold.

"Drop your shield, Nathan," Grant whispered. "We're on the same side here."

Nathan hesitated before letting his ward unravel.

When the last dryad had licked the final drops of the liquid from the oak leaf, the potentate returned it to Grant. He accepted it with a bow of his head, then rose and tucked the leaf back into the pouch at his waist. Only then did he address the dryad leader.

"Please, tell me what has scared you."

"A spriggan." Her voice rustled like dry leaves shaken together, and it took a moment for her words to register.

Cold dread plummeted through my stomach. Beside me, Grant turned to stone, his captain's mask sliding into place.

"A spriggan? Here? How close?" Nathan spun, as if expecting to find one creeping up behind him.

"Stay calm," Grant ordered.

"Maybe you don't understand the severity of the situation." Nathan's voice escalated in volume. "A spriggan will kill everything in its path. There's no stopping it. This entire grove, the forest, the city! The only option is fire, but even that might not kill—"

Grant clapped a patch of air over Nathan's babbling mouth. The writer's eyes bulged, then darted to check our surroundings. A forest of spears had been primed, each aimed at Nathan's throat, and trickles of wood element seeped from the oaks, coalescing into ominous magical clubs.

"I am well aware of the severity of the situation," Grant said, though nothing in his tone or body language indicated he felt threatened by the dryads. He turned to address the potentate. "Fire inside the dryads' grove is not the answer. I have another way of stopping a spriggan."

"You do?" I blurted out.

Ferocious, resilient, and bordering on unstoppable, spriggans demolished any living creature or plant in their paths. The dryads wouldn't be able to flee either; they couldn't abandon the trees to which their lives were bound. If a spriggan lurked close enough to the grove for the dryads to identify it, it was close enough to wipe out the entire Emerald Crown population. The last reported encounter with a spriggan had been a decade earlier on the East Coast, and it had decimated over a thousand acres before being stopped. Destroying it had required the combined efforts of three FPD units. Spriggans were also so rare their race teetered on the brink of extinction, and yet Grant miraculously possessed a mysterious weapon powerful enough to bring this monster down.

"You, alone, can stop a spriggan?" I couldn't disguise my disbelief.

Grant didn't look away from Potentate Heartwood. "I know of a way."

Nathan finally had the wherewithal to detach Grant's silencing spell using a flick of earth magic, and he pushed forward, stopping just short of getting in the captain's face. "Show us."

"I don't have it on me." For the first time, Grant's confidence cracked. It was only the flick of his tongue across his lips, but the tiny gesture betrayed him.

"Where is it?" I asked.

"In Beldame Zipporah's clutches."

My heart sank.

"The harpy?!" Nathan jabbed his fingers through his dark hair and fisted them, tugging hard enough to jiggle his ears. "She won't give anything to anyone. Not without exacting her fee—usually a body part or two. Shards and splinters, we're in deep trouble!"

"I could use your help," Grant said, surprisingly addressing Nathan and me.

"Oh no, that's way outside the parameters of this—"

"I want you both to return to Terra Haven and contact my squad," Grant said, overriding Nathan's protests.

"Done!" Nathan turned as if expecting to immediately escape the clearing, but the dryads surrounding us pulled short his retreat.

"It doesn't take two people to send a message," I said. I wasn't going to miss out on meeting Beldame Zipporah. I'd never chance a solo pilgrimage to the notorious harpy, and I'd never get a safer opportunity than in the company of the strongest elemental I knew. Plus, I was determined to go wherever the story took me.

"Have your brains been addled?" Nathan hissed. "You're a reporter, not a fighter. This is the problem with your lack of experience in the field. You're so intent on the story, you haven't figured out how to keep yourself separate from it. Leave the dangerous stuff to the professionals. Don't forget the first rule of journalism: Don't make yourself a part of your own story."

"I thought the first rule was to follow every lead." I folded my arms across my chest and switched my glare to the captain when he looked as if he would support Nathan's protests. "We're wasting time."

Grant studied my face. "Fine. Nathan will go alone."

Nathan shrugged, the gesture saying he'd done his part to save me from myself, and he would walk away with a clean conscience. Grant gave Nathan the communication signature of the base where his squad could be contacted, then sent the writer on his way. The dryads parted, and Nathan minced through the narrow opening, then bolted down Wicker Road toward Terra Haven without a backward glance. The trees lining the road quietly observed his passing.

"Will he follow through or just run?" Grant asked.

"He'll follow through. He wants the story."

If I'd run away with so much riding on this story, I never would have been able to live with myself, but the thought of encountering Zipporah—and then a spriggan!—made my knees quiver. I corralled my anxiety and buried it beneath a heaping pile of curiosity, pulling to the forefront the question that guided every story I wrote: What would my readers want to know?

"Why didn't you send an air message? It would have

been a lot faster." For anyone else, catapulting an air message across several miles would have been too taxing for their magical abilities, but I'd seen Grant's power in action. If he had wanted to, he could have gotten a message straight to his squad.

"Because at least this way one of you is getting to safety." He turned away to confer with the potentate.

I snapped my mouth shut and concentrated on collapsing my camera and tucking it safely back in my bag.

"Why does Grant think Beldame Zipporah will have a weapon to fight the spriggan?" Quinn whispered. "And why did Nathan act like she's worse than a spriggan?"

I crouched next to him to keep our conversation private. "Zipporah's an elemental harpy. Unlike most of her species, all the powers of her human half are intact, and it's said she's horribly powerful. She lives deep in the forest, far from anyone, but her reputation is near legendary. She's a trader and collector of unique and illegal objects, and she preys on the desperate. It's rumored that whatever you want, she can get it for you, but Nathan was right: She always exacts a price."

"How dangerous is she?"

"Deadly. But we'll be with the estimable captain, so no harm will befall us." I hoped I wasn't lying to Quinn.

"A direct assault will be suicide."

Grant's firm declaration snapped my head up. A cluster of larger dryads had gathered behind the potentate, the true warriors of the gentle race. They formed a half circle in front of the captain.

"The spriggan will reach Colden Creek before nightfall. We will not stand aside while our young are murdered," Potentate Heartwood said.

"I'm saying your strategy is flawed, not that you should

give up. The spriggan is stronger than all of you combined. If you insist on a straightforward attack, you will perish and it won't even slow the spriggan. Your sacrifices will mean nothing, and your children will die."

Grant spoke the truth, but the dryad warriors didn't want to hear it. A torrent of angry barks, chirps, and hisses flew through their ranks, and more than one warrior jabbed her spear menacingly in Grant's direction. The potentate's soft warble cut through their chatter, silencing them. She didn't immediately speak, though, exchanging another minute of mute eye contact with Grant. I fidgeted, urgency tingling at the base of my spine, and I had to bite my cheek to resist butting in and speeding up the conversation.

"What do you propose?" she finally asked.

"Allow me to defeat the spriggan," Grant said.

"We cannot wait—"

"I wouldn't expect you to. I need you to keep the spriggan occupied and prevent it from advancing. Hassle, harry, and distract it until I come back from Zipporah's, but don't try to attack it directly."

The potentate took her time mulling over his words before nodding. "We will try your method."

She signaled the dryads clustered around her, and they departed, melting into the forest beyond the meadow. More than half the dryads remained, each clutching a weapon. How many of them would pit their lives against the spriggan?

"Thank you, Potentate Heartwood." Grant's diplomatic serenity hardened into a granite mask as he turned to me. "We need to move quickly, Kylie. Link with me."

From my crouched position, Grant looked like a giant. I stood and straightened my bag on my shoulder. Grant and I had linked our magic before, but only as part of a larger group. A two-person link was far more intimate, and I collected my magic self-consciously. A person did not make it into the ranks of the Federal Pentagon Defense without being a full-spectrum pentacle potential, meaning Grant could wield all the elements at full strength. My skills ran toward air and to a lesser extent wood and fire, but my abilities with earth and water were limited. Compared to Grant, they were downright pathetic.

"Any day now, Kylie."

I glanced around at the dryads' anxious nut-brown faces and stopped dithering. Linking required collecting an equal level of each element into a single cohesive bundle. It would have worked with a thimbleful of each of the five elements, but pride made me draw as much water and earth as I could hold, then match their levels with air, fire, and wood. I passed this knot of magic to Grant, and he absorbed it into his own, bridging our magic into one.

As if I had linked with a gargoyle, his magic opened vast and powerful between us, as accessible to me as it was to him. However, unlike the pure enhancement of a gargoyle, Grant's magic contained the flavor of his personality and abilities all blended into a riveting magical signature. The sensual, crackling energy of a powerful thunderstorm rolled across my senses, sparking down my nerve endings. I muffled my gasp. His magic was everything that the man himself promised, and it was breathtakingly sexy.

When Grant opened himself to Quinn's enhancement, the sensation doubled, and I closed my eyes, basking in the midst of a wild storm, safe and supercharged at the same time.

"Anchor yourself," Grant said, his voice oddly loud. "Find your magic within the link, find your signature, and steady yourself. Just like in a group link, you need to remain separate while being part of the whole."

I suppressed a smile, grateful that he had mistaken my foolish indulgence as a loss of magical control, not an unfurling of my libido. Our magic was remarkably compatible but in no way mirrored, and I had no trouble separating myself from him. Nevertheless, I pulled back a smidgen on the link, pretending to collect myself before I opened my eyes.

Grant stood so close I wondered if he had thought he might have to prop me up. I gave him a bright smile and stepped away from him, throttling the split-second impulse to fake a faint just to have him catch me.

"I'm anchored."

Grant narrowed his eyes at me, and I wondered if he suspected the truth. Then he turned to the potentate. "We will need the most direct path possible to Zipporah's nest. Time is of the essence."

The trees rustled and creaked, branches shifting and twisting to open an almost arrow-straight line due east.

"Wow!" Quinn whispered.

I wished I hadn't already packed my camera. I'd known the dryads controlled all the trees in Emerald Crown Grove, not just those to which they were bonded—the violent, restless oaks along Wicker Road had proved as much—but I'd had no idea the extent of their authority.

Grant seemed to have expected nothing less, and while Quinn and I had gaped at the forest's transformation, he had been busy creating a platform of air. Hardly larger than the rug I had flown through the city on, it hovered a few inches above the ground. However, it supported the captain's weight without flexing when he stepped on it.

"Let's go." Grant held a hand out to me.

"Couldn't you make it a bit bigger?" Even with us both standing, I would have to be pressed up against him to fit on the platform.

"I could, but I'd rather conserve my strength. If you would prefer, you can wait here."

I slapped my hand into his and climbed behind him onto the see-through platform.

5

Situating my feet behind Grant's, I wrapped my arms loosely around his waist and vacillated over my hand placement: Gripping his belt seemed logical until I realized how low that positioned my hands, but anything else made me feel like I was copping a feel of him through the supple material of his uniform. Grant solved the issue by pressing my fluttering hands against his rock-hard abs. His muscles bunched beneath my fingers and I stilled. Our feet had to touch for me to fit on the platform behind him, and I held myself stiffly so my chest didn't brush his backside.

"Stay close and keep us boosted," Grant instructed Quinn.

The gargoyle nodded and launched into the air. This time the oaks let him pass freely, and when he cleared the shade of the meadow, the sun made his citrine body almost too bright to look at.

"Have you ever flown on an air platform?" Grant asked.

I shook my head, then realized he couldn't see, but he

must have felt the movement, because he added, "Bend your knees and sink into your center of gravity. Hold on."

The platform shifted beneath my feet, and I clutched Grant's shirt to save myself from tumbling off the back. I settled into my stance and loosened my grip, reestablishing the gap between our bodies. We glided through the crowd of dryads, who parted like the trees to let us pass. Grant tugged magic through the link, drawing on my power as he increased our speed. I followed the lines of his magic down to the platform, studying how he had created the solid sheet of air beneath us and how he maintained it as we traveled. The weave was ridiculously complex, but I thought I might be able to re-create it, if on a much smaller scale. I'd never be able to support myself, let alone two people, with just my own magic.

On the back end of the platform, spiraling turbines of air laced with delicate strands of fire propelled us, similar to those on Jolene's flying carpet, but far more sophisticated and efficient.

Grant revved up the turbines and the platform jetted forward. I cinched my arms tight around him when my balance tipped backward, plastering myself to him for stability. We rocked in unison, but Grant's sturdy legs stabilized us, and I didn't dare relax my grip again. In my peripheral vision, oaks flashed past faster than shutter clicks. My loose hair whipped in the wind, stinging my cheeks and eyes, and I pressed my face into the subtle hollow between Grant's shoulder blades, using a trickle of air to wrap the blond strands behind my ear and hold them in place. When I looked for Quinn, I found him gliding above us, keeping up as easily as if he were attached by a kite string.

Grant's scent swirled around me, a delicious aroma of sun-warmed skin spiced with subtle notes of energized ozone, the by-product of his magic. I inhaled a second, heady breath, and my thoughts stuttered. I'd entertained a fair share of foolish fantasies of being this close to Grant, but in them, I'd always been held in his arms, not the other way around. I hadn't known what I was missing. Though I'd seen the outline of his figure through his uniform, I hadn't realized quite how solid he was until now. His stomach flexed underneath my hands and his backside bunched against my stomach each time he made a minute balance adjustment, every inch of him enticingly firm.

What I wouldn't give to see this man naked.

I mentally shook my head at myself. Not only was Grant well out of my league, but also I had more important things to do than contemplate his delicious body against mine.

Keeping my movements to a minimum and corralling my thoughts back onto a professional track, I tilted my head up and shouted into the wind, "When did you become aware of a problem in Emerald Crown Grove?"

His ribs expanded in a sigh before he answered. "An hour before you showed up."

Considering it'd taken me a half hour to get to the forest, my scout had been recording the merchant's frightened words around the same time Grant had learned about the riled dryads. Not too bad, though I made a mental note to expand the range of my scouts beyond the borders of Terra Haven. If not for the merchant returning to town, I would have missed this story completely.

"The dryads chased at least one person from Wicker Road, and I nearly got trampled by another wagon on my way in. If they were trying to get everyone safely away from the spriggan, that doesn't explain why they looked ready to kill us."

Grant didn't respond, and I realized I'd failed to present

an actual question. Rolling my eyes, I added, "Why did they treat us like the enemy at first? What did you mean when you said they were 'frenzied'?"

"It's their defense. When their grove is threatened, it triggers a berserker response in the dryads. Once frenzied, they perceive every outsider as an enemy, and they can be shockingly vicious. We're fortunate the potentate held them in check long enough for me to calm them."

"How did you know to bring the herbal theriaca?"

"I'm good at my job."

"What was in the theriaca?"

"A soup of minerals and algae. It's very nutritious for the dryads as well as mentally clarifying."

"Have you met Potentate Heartwood before?"

"Yes."

I resisted the urge to drum my fingers on his stomach in frustration. I'd interviewed the captain before, and I knew he took a not-so-secret delight in being taciturn with journalists. Or maybe just with me.

Mindful of the cramp forming in my neck, I discarded a dozen questions about the dryads. I could follow up with Grant later, perhaps to write a second, smaller exposé on the dryad community. He wouldn't be able to dodge my questions forever, and however today's events panned out, Dahlia would likely be pleased with a follow-up article.

But first I had to write *this* story.

"What is this mysterious weapon that enables you to stop a spriggan single-handedly?"

"Landewednack dragon's breath."

"I've never heard of it."

Grant grunted.

"Is a Landewednack a type of dragon?" I tried to picture

a dragon tolerating being shackled in a harpy's nest, but my imagination failed me.

"Landewednack is a place," Grant said.

He swerved to avoid a majestic oak, and I tightened my arms around him when my balance tipped. I decided to wait to pester for ancillary details until we were on more stable ground and stuck to the most important questions.

"Are you sure Beldame Zipporah will have the dragon's breath?"

"Positive."

"Why?"

"You don't live as long as she has without planning for every eventuality."

"So you don't actually know if she has it? You only *think* she does?"

"I'm not going to talk in circles with you. I know I make this look easy, Kylie, but it takes a certain amount of concentration to hold all these weaves together and keep us moving."

I closed my mouth and considered our predicament. When I tilted my head up to shout my next question, Grant's ribs expanded in another sigh that I pretended not to notice.

"When the spriggan demolishes its way through the forest, Zipporah will be in as much danger as everyone else. Shouldn't she give us the dragon's breath?"

Grant shook his head. "Zipporah gives away nothing for free."

"But we'll be protecting her nest, too."

"The spriggan isn't threatening her nest."

"Not yet, but it will."

"It only *might*. If the spriggan does, she would have no problem killing it, but until she's directly threatened, she won't act. Zipporah doesn't care about anything else the

spriggan destroys or whether it wipes out the entire population of dryads and their trees. We care, and she will use that
to exact the highest price she can."

I wanted to protest, but arguing with Grant wouldn't
change Zipporah's reputation.

The trees zipped by at a dizzying rate, and I closed my
eyes. I tried to enjoy the feel of Grant's strong body pressed
against mine, but trepidation nipped at me, making it
impossible to relax. After far too long alone with my own
thoughts, Grant brought the platform to a halt. I peered
around him. We had arrived.

The harpy's nest roosted atop a mammoth spire of boulders far above the loamy soil of the forest. An unnatural
break in the trees created a clearing extending fifty feet
around the base, and Grant stopped us within the shade of
the trees. I squinted against the sun to study the nest at the
top. From here, it resembled an overturned beaver's dam,
twisted trunks used the way normal birds would use twigs to
build a colossal bowl. An even taller, jagged rock bleached
completely white by the sun jutted from the back of
the nest.

The breeze shifted, carrying a foul odor. I amended my
assessment: That wasn't sun damage on the rock. It
was feces.

Ew.

Grant had signaled Quinn to drop down along our trail
under the tree canopy several minutes earlier, and the
gargoyle coasted to a sliding stop next to us. I stepped off
the platform, and Grant dissolved it and the link between us
at the same time. My vision tunneled dark around the
edges, and I bent forward to brace my hands on my knees.
My back popped and I flexed cramped fingers. When Quinn
withdrew his enhancement, leaving me alone inside my

magic, I forced myself straight. After having insisted on accompanying Grant, I refused to let him blame me for slowing him down. Fortunately, he wasn't paying attention to me.

"This is as far as you go, Quinn," he said.

"But I can help."

"Zipporah would love to get her hands on a gargoyle, and she wouldn't be inclined to let go. I can't protect you from her, not alone, and the last thing we need to contend with is a gargoyle-enhanced harpy."

"I wouldn't amplify her magic," Quinn protested.

"Zipporah is a master at coercion. And unfortunately, we both know there are ways to force you. It's best if we avoid tempting her at all."

Quinn's wings slumped. I could tell he wanted to put on a brave face and insist on going with us, but he'd been used and abused for his magic-enhancing abilities before, and those emotional scars ran deep.

"You were an enormous help in getting us here quickly," I said, drawing the gargoyle's attention. If I felt this tired after having Quinn's boost, I could only imagine how much more fatigued I would be if he hadn't accompanied us. "We'll need your help getting to the spriggan, too. But right now, Grant and I have got this. Stay here, and stay hidden, and we'll be back for you."

"Better yet, Kylie, you're staying here with Quinn."

"No, I'm not."

"Yes, you are."

I planted my hands on my hips. "Why did you bring me this far if you planned to ditch me at the foot of Beldame Zipporah's nest?"

"Because I couldn't trust you to stay put back at the meadow. You'd have either followed me here or trailed the dryads to the spriggan. This was the safest option for all of us."

He thought of himself as my babysitter. How flattering.

"I guess I should stay here, then," I said, choosing my words carefully.

I surveyed the unnatural pile of massive rocks. The harpy must have carried each gigantic boulder to this location to assemble her aberrant stone perch. It stretched high into the sky, well above the canopy. Somewhere up there, Zipporah lurked out of sight. Heights didn't scare me, but the harpy did.

"What are you waiting for?" I asked Grant.

He squinted at me, as if he could read my thoughts if he stared hard enough. Finally, he said, "Stay in the shadows of these trees. The harpy has keen vision, and I won't be here to protect you if she spots you."

With one last dubious glance over his shoulder at me, Grant jogged across the barren ground between the tree line and the rock spire, and out of sight behind the boulders.

"Are you really going to stay with me?" Quinn asked.

I shook my head. Missing my chance to meet Beldame Zipporah wasn't an option. Besides, Grant would never tell me about his meeting in enough detail to satisfy me, and a good reporter got firsthand accounts.

"Promise me you'll stay hidden," I said.

Quinn nodded, his wide mouth curled in a deep frown.

I waited another forty-five seconds, then tiptoed after Grant.

6

I climbed the jumbled boulders cautiously, concerned as much with my footing as with attracting Grant's attention. Ideally, I'd catch up with him near the top. We both knew Grant didn't have the authority to curtail my movements in Emerald Crown Grove, and he had even less legal right to dictate my actions atop Beldame Zipporah's mountain, but that wouldn't stop him from trying to order me around. If I timed it right, he'd have no choice but to allow me to accompany him to the harpy's nest, and I wouldn't even have to argue with him.

I scrambled my way around the mountain, angling upward in a long, spiral pattern, following Grant's footsteps in the dust. Zipporah had assembled the hunks of granite and feldspar with a focus on stability, not ease of foot traffic. If anything, she'd probably designed it to be more difficult to scale.

The sun baked my body and the mountain with equal ambivalence, and the dark rocks singed my fingertips when precarious sections of the trail forced me to cling to stone handholds for balance. Sweat trickled down my spine and plastered my shirt to my body beneath the strap of my bag. After the first turn around the mountain without spotting Grant, I paused in the shade of an overhanging boulder and surveyed my progress. I hadn't climbed even halfway up the mountain, but one slip from this height and I'd take a bone-breaking plummet to the ragged rocks below—or the fall would kill me. I pushed the thought from my mind and resumed my climb.

My foot hit a patch of scree, and I slipped. Flinging out a hand to grab the rock next to me for balance, I regained my footing, but I couldn't stop the mini-landslide cascading down the mountain, or the racket it created. I froze, listening for Grant. I hadn't heard him once, and when he didn't appear now, I couldn't decide whether to be relieved or alarmed. He must have been farther ahead of me than I'd anticipated. I needed to pick up my pace.

I scrambled up two smaller stones, straightening to trot along a path no wider than my foot, clinging to the grainy surface of a tall rock for balance. When I looked up, Grant loomed in front of me.

I yelped and lost my grip. Teetering, I windmilled my arms. Grant's hand shot out and grabbed the strap of my bag, hauling me to safety on the flat rock next to him. I started to thank him but thought better of it when I took in his thunderous expression.

"I told you not to follow me."

I twisted my arm from his grasp. "You keep forgetting that I have a job to do, just like you."

"Our jobs are nothing alike. Mine is to defend the citizens of Terra Haven from all manner of deadly threats. Your job is to fill column space. If you don't do your job, the paper fluffs a title's font size to take up the empty space. If I don't do my job, people die."

"So you've got strong magic and were born with a body that could build big muscles. Good for you. That doesn't make what you do any more important than what I do."

"You can't be serious." Grant crossed his arms, chest inflated, doing a great impersonation of a puffed-up wall.

My spine snapped straight and I pushed into his personal space. If he thought he could use his larger stature to intimidate me, he didn't know me that well. "There's more than one way to protect and defend people," I snarled. "You can spend your time scurrying around saving individuals; I prefer to disseminate information, raise awareness of problems, and save thousands of lives by arming the citizens of Terra Haven with the knowledge to save themselves."

"How noble of you. But explain to me how serving yourself up to Zipporah like a clumsy, brain-dead goat is going to 'save' the readers of the *Chronicle*."

"You act like there's a chance the harpy will notice me. All I'll have to do is stand behind your colossal ego, and she'll never even know I'm there."

Grant growled my name, and a shiver slid down my abdomen. I disguised my reaction behind a scowl. Stepping back, I crossed my arms, mirroring his posture. He blocked the path to higher ground, so I was forced to crane my head back to glare at him.

"Obtaining the Landewednack dragon's breath is a part of the story," I said.

"At best, it's a footnote."

"It could be the most important part."

"It's not, and I won't let you add to Zipporah's notoriety. The last thing we need are more idiots scaling this mountain, feeding themselves to the harpy."

"Too bad it's not up to you."

His fists bunched against his biceps in an impressive

display of strength that strained the sleeves of his shirt. "So help me, I'll tie you to this rock and leave you until I'm done with the spriggan unless you—"

"I need this story," I blurted out. "If I bring my editor the headline story today, she'll send me to the everlasting tree. This is the only way I can attend the blooming. Plus, the seed drop will be the biggest story the paper has covered in decades."

Grant relaxed fractionally. "So it's not a rumor? The tree is blooming?"

"Our gryphon scout confirmed it this morning, and that's when my editor issued the challenge for a top-notch story."

His dark eyes scanned my features. "What would you have done if the spriggan hadn't shown up today?"

"There have been thefts at the docks. I would have done some investigating." I shifted, unsure if I could trust this quieter, inquisitive Grant.

"And Nathan?"

"He wants to win, and he's not above stealing my story to do it. He wouldn't have known anything was happening in the grove if he hadn't been there when my rum— when Quinn broke the news." I hoped I'd caught my flub quick enough to fool Grant. He didn't know about my rumor scouts, and I preferred to keep it that way. "I've been monitoring the dryads for a few weeks, and now Nathan's trying to take point on this story simply because he's a senior writer. I'm not letting him have it."

"Okay." Grant glanced up the mountain, then back at me. "But you still haven't given me a reason you can't wait with Quinn. If you come with me, you'll only make things worse."

"I'm not completely useless or the imbecile you make me out to be."

"Prove it. Go back down before—"

I sensed the magic swell behind him before I saw it. A cyclone of air and metallic blades rounded the craggy incline, barreling straight for us. Sparks flew when the blades nicked the rocks, and I flinched away from the ricochet of granite shrapnel. Grant cursed and grabbed my arm, positioning me between the rock wall and him.

"Link. Now!"

I fumbled to collect equal levels of magic, eyes fixated on the vicious storm. If the serrated cyclone reached us, it'd slice through bone as easily as flesh. The link I passed Grant trembled but stabilized when he snatched hold of it. He folded it into his magic and seized the elements without waiting for me to adjust. My internal compass tilted, and I braced a hand against the rock to stay upright. By the time I regained my bearings, a ward of earth and fire encapsulated us. The cyclone shredded the outer edges of the ward, and Grant drew heavily on my magic to strengthen it. The sharp blades within the cyclone continued to whittle away at his protective barrier, but at a slower rate.

"What is that?"

"A deterrent."

Thank you, Mr. Obvious. "I meant, what are those sharp objects?" Grant's ward should have been enough to deflect and dull normal blades, but these continued to eat away at our combined magic.

"Feathers. Let's go."

He dragged me two steps down the mountain before I realized he intended to take me back to the forest. I dug in my heels—not that Grant noticed or slowed. The deadly cyclone accelerated around us, reversing course to throw its full force in the path of our retreat, dicing into the ward. When we backpedaled up the mountain, the assault slackened, though it didn't fully let up.

"The only way to go is up," I said, trying not to sound pleased.

Grant's scowl should have bored straight through the mountain. His jaw locked as he shoved back down the boulders, his hand a bruising vise on my wrist. Again, the cyclone's attack escalated, diminishing when we reversed course.

"She's herding us," I said.

"And whittling away our strength. I bet this is designed to pressure us. Zipporah wants us worn out by the time we reach her nest. It's smart." He released my arm and gave me a flat stare. "Keep up."

We climbed, our steps nearly on top of each other, the ward forcing us to stay close enough that our shoulders and thighs bumped each other. More than once, Grant hoisted me across terrain too narrow for us to travel side by side, and he carried me with all the effort and reverence he would a sack of dirty laundry. The cyclone never relented, rotating to attack from different directions, the ferocity of the blades waxing and waning with no rhythm, making it impossible to relax our guards for even a few seconds. Grant was right: Beldame Zipporah was softening our defenses to make us more vulnerable, and our only recourse was to keep moving.

My thighs burned from the perpetual climb, my footsteps turning clumsy from the exertion and Grant's heavy reliance on my magic to strengthen the ward. He may have resented my presence, but he did actually need me.

The lethal whirlwind chased us to the base of the nest and then dissipated. Freed, metallic-edged feathers whistled through the air, embedding in the wooden limbs of the nest in staccato thumps and sparking off the granite boulders before clattering down the mountain. Those that struck our ward bounced harmlessly to our feet, slid down the uneven surface of the rock, and disappeared. I shuddered. Without the ward, we both would have been decapitated.

Grant dropped the link between us without warning, and I sagged against the nest, pretending to be engrossed in studying one of the feathers while I collected myself. My magic flexed with the lassitude of an overworked muscle when I tested it. I sucked in a deep breath, instantly regretting it. The stench that had wafted down to the forest floor hung in a thick, cloying reek here.

When my legs could hold me without shaking, I stepped back from the nest to examine it. This close, I couldn't take in its entirety. Easily larger than my studio apartment in both depth and width, the nest protruded from the harpy-made mountain in a network of rotting oaks and pines, all the gaps between tree trunks stuffed with detritus. If a bird and a rat had come together to make a nest, this would have been it, except this nest could fit a gryphon and have room left over. Just how big was Beldame Zipporah?

Grant surveyed the forest below us, a hand held to his brow to shield the sunlight from his eyes. Somewhere out there a spriggan ravaged the landscape, but we couldn't see it from here.

I should have let it go, but I couldn't stop myself from saying, "Good thing I came along. You wouldn't have made it without me."

"Mmm-hmm."

Mmm-hmm? How about a thank you! "Even big, bad FPD warriors require help every once in a while," I prodded.

"Is that so?" Grant finally turned to look at me, his expression oddly smug.

"You used my magic like a crutch. You wouldn't have made it halfway...alone..."

His self-satisfied smile widened as I trailed off. Despite the steep climb, he'd barely broken a sweat. I might have attributed his restful appearance to his phenomenal physique, but I was in pretty good shape myself, and the climb had worn me out. With the cyclone requiring all of the magic in the link to hold it at bay, he should have been tired from his magical exertions alone.

I crossed my arms and tapped my right foot, suspicion sparking irritation. "Did we even need to link?"

"What do you think?"

I thought I wanted to wipe that arrogant expression off his face. Why hadn't I questioned how heavily he'd leaned on my magic? He was a *captain* in the FPD; unaided, he should have been more than a match for that storm.

"You used me!"

"You broke your promise to stay in the forest."

"I never made any such promise!"

Grant tilted his head, and I could practically hear him replaying our conversation. "No, you were careful not to promise, weren't you?" He refocused on me, and I flinched under his hard-eyed glare. "You don't give a damn about my orders, and you've proven you don't trust my judgment. Since you insisted on coming along, unwanted, why should I have wasted my energy protecting you?"

I sputtered, a dozen rebuttals snarling together on my tongue.

"I could've gotten the weapon from the harpy with only one favor." Furious heat broke through his stony mask, and he leaned close, pitching his voice low. "Now it'll cost one from each of us, unless we get lucky. You should be grateful I saved my energy, because you're going to need my protection against the real danger."

"Maybe I wouldn't need your protection if you hadn't *stolen* all my magic." I wanted to scream, but I matched his volume, reminded that even though we couldn't see Beldame Zipporah, she could be listening to our conversation from atop her nest.

"Even when you're at full strength, you can't overpower me. What could you possibly do to protect yourself if the harpy attacked you?"

I glared at him. Nothing I could say would help my argument.

Grant slapped a small item into my palm. "Swallow this. We need to get moving before she sics another attack cyclone on us."

I examined the packet stamped with the FPD's logo, my hands shaking with indignation. "What is it?"

"A pick-me-up. I can't let you confront Zipporah in your current state."

"Maybe you should have thought about that before you decided to teach me a lesson," I ground out.

"I did. That should tide you over."

I longed to throw the packet at his face; instead, I ripped it open and shoved the tiny tablet into my mouth. It began to dissolve instantly, releasing a brackish, bitter flavor across my tongue. Swallowing convulsively, I forced the tablet down, not breaking my glare from Grant.

"Let's go." He turned and began to climb through the woven branches of the nest without waiting for me.

A tingle of energy spread from my stomach outward, chasing away the weariness in my muscles. When I reached for them, the elements leapt to my grasp. Still, my legs wobbled when I climbed the first protruding trunk, and I paused to give my muscles time to steady. A feather gleamed at eye level, and I tugged it free on a whim, cutting my fingers on the sharp shaft. Pinching the feather gingerly between the thumb and forefinger of my opposite hand, I shook away the sting of the cuts while I twisted the feather in the sunlight. The shaft shimmered with a metallic gleam, and the individual hairs comprising the vanes protruded like the slender tongs of a metal comb. Individually, they were so weak I could snap them off, but collectively, they formed an edge as sharp as a chef's knife. Tugging my journal from my bag, I carefully closed the feather inside it, feeling braver for making a souvenir of the harpy's former weapon.

Grant waited for me, all traces of anger replaced by his stern captain's mask. The moment I caught up, he resumed his climb. I followed close, using the same foot placements and handholds as Grant, and did my best to avoid putting my hand in any dried feces or scratching myself on half-rotten branches. We couldn't climb directly up the face of the nest and were forced along a circumlocutory route that took us out over the drop-off. Peering straight down at the sun-scorched clearing beneath the nest shot a tingle of weightlessness through my limbs, and I clutched my perch for balance against a wash of vertigo. When I had scanned the horizon for the spriggan, I hadn't been paying attention to how high we'd climbed. From this vantage, the massive oaks of the forest below us looked as small as shrubs. If I lost my footing, the drop would kill me.

After that, I spent less time worrying about accidentally touching poop and more about my purchase on the inter-locking branches.

When we finally reached the lip of the nest and straightened, I gagged and clutched Grant's arm to stay upright. Layers of feces and carrion filled the deep nest to the brim, overflowing down the far side, and flies coated the air. I cast a quick eye over the copious remains, searching for human skeletons and trying not to see the maggots writhing like animated puss in the rotting meat. I didn't spot any telltale skulls, but I could see only the top layer.

The harpy herself was missing.

At the back of the nest, a deep cavern tunneled through several large boulders, and the sunlight didn't penetrate more than a foot into its mysterious depths. Nevertheless, I leaned forward, heart pounding in my ears, squinting to catch my first glimpse of Beldame Zipporah.

This is how it must feel to stand at the precipice of a dragon's den.

"Do not, for any reason, touch your magic," Grant whispered, his lips barely moving. "Do not do or say anything to attract her attention."

His upturned gaze focused on the top of the rock pile, not the cavern, and I followed his line of sight.

If the harpy had been perched at the pinnacle earlier, she would have been visible from the ground; she was that huge. Her eaglelike body stood as tall as a human, the individual golden-brown feathers of her wings longer than my arms, the leathery toes of her feet thicker than my thighs. Atop this massive body, her human head protruded, an eerie, alien meld of woman and avian predator. When her rapacious stare locked on me, adrenaline flooded my system, and it took all my willpower not to scramble back over the edge of the nest and flee down the mountain.

Releasing an earsplitting cry, Beldame Zipporah launched from her perch, a stream of excrement splattering the rock behind her. She flapped twice and circled the spire, her wings filling the sky, her massive body blocking out the sun. Twisting midair, she dove for us, talons extended.

Grant's hand brushed mine, stilling me when instinct insisted I cower and hide. On quaking knees, I held my ground. At the last second, she flapped her wings and bent her legs, sailing so close overhead that her tail feathers missed Grant's forehead by inches. The wind of her passing whipped my hair into my face, but my fear-locked limbs held me rigid. If she had wanted to, she could have wrapped her long claws around Grant's broad torso and had room to spare in her grip. She could have grabbed us each, one human per foot, and tossed us from her nest without straining herself. My heart knocked against my chest and a fine tremor scuttled from my spine to my fingers.

Grant didn't so much as flinch.

Zipporah landed on the rim across from us, hopping around to face us. Her stench punched the back of my throat and clogged my esophagus. I'd gotten a close-up view of the harpy's underside caked with her own fecal matter, and her wings stirred an even worse odor from the depths of the nest. Bile crawled up my throat, and I swallowed it back down.

The nest, which had seemed spacious moments earlier, shrank to claustrophobic dimensions. Trapped atop this mountain, cut off from any means of escape or any place to hide, we were vulnerable, and Zipporah knew it.

7

"An FPD air elemental and a . . . Did you bring me a child?" The harpy cocked her head from side to side in predaceous curiosity, the movement more reminiscent of a bird than a human. Darkened by sun, with tiny ears, a sharp nose, and piercing eyes that missed nothing, Beldame Zipporah exhibited little trace of humanity. Short brown hair slicked her scalp and trailed down her neck to meet the feathers on her back, but her chest remained grotesquely bare, sun-damaged leathery flesh stretched across her prominent breastbone, with two unsightly deflated folds of skin in place of human breasts.

"It's been far too long since I savored the tender flesh of an infantile human. My dear man, you must require an extraordinary gift from me."

I didn't shift under her scrutiny; I couldn't. If I moved, my legs would buckle, even if I was almost certain she was playing off my fear. If she ate humans, I would've heard about it.

Unless no one had been left alive to bring the tales to Terra Haven.

Pain cracked down my dry throat when I attempted to swallow, and I wished I could take a deep breath to ground myself. I'd been confining myself to shallow inhalations, and even then, the omnipresent putridity coated my tongue.

"A spriggan threatens the forest," Grant said, not reacting to the harpy's taunts.

"Have you come to rescue me, human?" Zipporah snickered.

"I came to barter for Landewednack dragon's breath."

She lifted hairless eyebrows. "You're on the wrong continent."

My heart sank. She didn't have it. We'd come all this way and had done nothing but waste time. How much land had the spriggan ravaged while we'd been scaling this mountain? And worse, how would we stop it without the dragon's breath?

Grant crossed his arms, unperturbed. "Which is why I've come to you," he said.

"And if I don't have it?"

"Then you must be an impostor, and I'll chase you from this nest, earning the real Beldame Zipporah's gratitude."

The harpy stilled, holding Grant's gaze. Then she threw back her head and cackled. A breeze ruffled her scalp, exposing downy feathers rather than human hair. "As tempting as it is to let you try to expel me from my home, I must confess I do possess the dragon's breath."

My knees weakened with relief, and I locked them so I didn't sag.

Zipporah leapt into the center of the nest, her nimbleness shocking for her size, and I startled. Her eyes snapped to me, a predator's excited gaze drawn to my fear-based reaction. When she exhaled, the rancid odor of rotten carrion rolled over me.

She flared her wings wide, the tips extending beyond the edges of the nest and the long feathers draping to the filthy basin, forming a wall in front of us. Along the arms of her wings, sunlight glinted on metal-sharp feathers, the likes of which had attacked us in the cyclone. The rest were normal eagle feathers, if an eagle had ever grown over five feet tall.

Eyes watering, I held my breath. I yearned to back up, but the drop-off hung a few steps behind us. She'd corralled us at the precipice, and all she had to do was hop forward to shove us to our deaths. I chanced a glance at Grant, for reassurance and guidance. Even he looked small standing this close to the harpy, but he remained relaxed, with no visible magic prepared.

"If I traded the dragon's breath to you, I would be defenseless," Zipporah said. "How do I know you won't trick me and wait until the spriggan has destroyed my nest before you kill it?"

"My name is Grant Monaghan. If you've heard of my deeds, you know I am a man of my word, and I promise to protect you."

Zipporah shivered dramatically, releasing a noxious wave of body odor before she folded her wings. "A human driven by honor and duty. Lucky me."

When her peculiar gaze locked on me, my body stiffened.

"And you, child? Are you the gargoyle healer I've heard runs around with the FPD now?"

A thrill of alarm skittered through me. She meant my best friend, but how had Mika attracted the attention of Beldame Zipporah? Had it been my own stories in the *Chronicle* about her? The last thing I had intended with those articles was to draw sordid attention to my friend.

"I am Kylie Grayson, a journalist with the *Terra Haven Chronicle*."

"Interesting." Zipporah's smile revealed surprisingly human teeth, though so dirty they matched her tan skin. "Why are *you* here?"

"Because she's nosy, like all reporters." Grant's tone held an admonishment for me. In my haste to distract Zipporah from Mika, I had revealed more than necessary about myself.

Grant tugged a coin pouch from his belt. From the way its sides bulged, it contained more than two months' rent. "Name your price."

Zipporah hopped backward with a flap of her wings. I dropped to a crouch to maintain my balance against the buffet of wind, straightening just as quickly and wiping my filthy hand on my pants, trying not to think about what I had touched or why it had been slimy between my fingers.

"I don't want your money," Zipporah said. "I want something more precious. I want a tiny piece of you." Her gaze roved suggestively to the crotch of Grant's pants, and she wriggled bald eyebrows at him.

"No games, Beldame Zipporah, or I'll leave. There are other ways to eliminate a spriggan."

The harpy cackled again. "Aren't you a tough one, *Captain*?" She emphasized his title, revealing she knew more about Grant than she had let on. His gray uniform with the elemental icon at the collar identified Grant as a member of an FPD squad, but nothing in his apparel specified his rank. "I'm sure you are used to getting all the best jobs, so I will accept your payment in humility and muscle: I will give you the dragon's breath once you've cleaned my nest."

I surveyed the sloppy heap, dismayed. It would take Grant hours to clean it. In the meantime, the spriggan would be devouring everything in its path, including the dryads and their trees.

Grant surprised me by beginning negotiations instead of rejecting her offer. He haggled over the definition of the nest, refining it down to only the parts within the wooden frame, not the cavern, and nothing beyond the rim of the nest. He stipulated that he would only remove bones and feces, not dirt, dander, or other matter deeper in the framework of the nest, nor could she add anything else to it as he worked. I never would have thought to negotiate those details, and Zipporah seemed disappointed that Grant hadn't been caught in her open-ended trap.

"Kylie will assist me—"

"No." Zipporah cut him off, her tone losing all traces of affability. "The deal is with you alone or you have no deal at all."

Grant pinched his lips together and nodded.

"Come, newspaper child. Let's get out of the way so the distinguished captain can get to work." The harpy used the tip of one wing to point toward the cavern.

I didn't need to see Grant's warning look to recognize the need for caution. I didn't want to leave his side. I definitely didn't want to go into the foreboding cave without him, but I made my feet move. Any delay could be costing a dryad its life.

Stumbling my way around the edge of the filthy nest, I gave myself a mental pep talk. *This will all make a great story. I'll have details no journalist at the* Chronicle *has ever obtained about Beldame Zipporah. This is exactly what I'd hoped for.*

But no matter which way I twisted my perspective, I couldn't shake the feeling that I was walking to my own doom.

8

Zipporah hopped to the cavern entrance, forcing me to stumble into the darkness. Tears leaked from my eyes as the stifling combination of excrement and rot amplified each other in the stagnant air. I wished I could use my arm to cover my nose, but I wasn't sure if doing so would offend the harpy. I squeezed to the wall, my nose slowly numbing and the urge to vomit receding.

Behind us, Grant formed shovels out of air and began tossing layers of offal and bones over the edge of the mountain. I waited to see if Zipporah would protest, but she nodded approvingly at his disposal methods.

"I keep the dragon's breath in the back," she said.

Leaning close, she spread a wing around me and hugged me to her grimy body. The metallic feathers along the arm of her wing bit into my neck, a sharp pain letting me know she had drawn blood. When she exerted pressure, I had no choice but to stagger deeper into the cavern with her. She took dainty steps, her head bobbing back and forth like a chicken's, her wing alternately cutting into me and backing off.

I wanted to run, but even if I could escape her long reach, I had nowhere to go in the dead-end cave. The best I could do was outpace her to avoid having my neck lacerated by her sharp feathers. The sun's bright rays receded, step by step, and I stumbled over items I couldn't see and didn't want to identify. Gradually, my eyes adjusted, aided by the soft glow of a few candles. They illuminated the back of the cave where unexpectedly smooth oval walls swelled twice as wide as the tunnel, all lined with handcrafted shelving from filthy floor to jagged ceiling. Hundreds of marvels adorned the shelves, each placed neatly beside the next with no particular importance given to any single item. Expensive copper chains of a kludde collar lay next to a chipped porcelain squirrel figurine that wouldn't have sold for more than a few pennies. I scanned the hoard of items for the dragon's breath, realizing only then that I had no clue what it looked like. It could have been any number of objects, including the three-bladed sword on the bottom shelf or the scythe etched in Scandinavian ruins on the far right or the coal-black wyvern figurine holding a lit candle—and I wished Zipporah would point it out to me so I could collect it and leave the cavern.

Zipporah herded me into the center of the room and stopped where her body blocked the exit. "We haven't discussed what you will give me in exchange for the dragon's breath."

The panic I'd been holding at bay shuddered through me, scattering my thoughts.

"You already agreed to give it to Grant," I hedged.

"Yes, but I did not agree to give it to *you*. Are you volunteering to stay here?" A hungry glint lit Zipporah's eyes.

I wiped sweaty palms against my hips. "What do you want?"

"You have nothing to give me. You're too scrawny to be of use for anything physical, and your magic is pathetic. The only thing you have to offer is your life."

Her curled foot shot forward, punching me in the solar plexus and knocking me to my back. The feces-encrusted floor broke my fall, but my head cracked against something hard, and my brain jarred inside my skull. My vision doubled. Before I recovered, Zipporah slammed her foot atop my gut, pinning me in place. Her back talon curled into the ground between my calves, two of her long front toes confined my upper arms, and her thick middle toe arced to rest its talon tip against the hollow of my throat. Instinctively, I clutched the talon and heaved, but my hands were too small to encircle the steel-hard claw, and I couldn't get any leverage with my biceps restrained. She crooked her toe. The sharp prick of her talon puncturing the delicate skin of my neck took a moment to penetrate my alarm, and I froze.

Frantic, I cycled through every spell I knew, seeking one that had a chance of freeing me faster than Zipporah could kill me. I came up blank. Any fire I could ignite, she could extinguish. Any punch of air I threw at her, she could dissipate. Her magic far outstripped mine, and even if I'd had the physical strength to grapple with her, a single flex of her toe would decapitate me. No one, not even Grant, would have been fast enough from this position.

"I . . . I have a camera. In my bag." My voice trembled. I had no money, and my half-used journal wasn't worth the paper it was printed on. The camera was my sole bartering option.

"A camera? Do you think your life is worth so little? Or are you insulting me by claiming Landewednack dragon's breath, the only known weapon against the spriggan, has so little value?"

"It's precious to me. I would be bereft without it."

"Do better," Zipporah barked.

My brain burbled with half-formed thoughts, terror a pounding pressure inside my skull. When I swallowed convulsively, the tip of the talon nicked my throat again. "I can write a story about you! I can make you famous."

Zipporah leaned down, compressing my stomach and chest, making it impossible to inhale. The harpy snapped her teeth in my face, and I flinched despite myself.

"There is no value in fame," she said. "Besides, I don't need more noxious humans crawling up my mountain."

A trickle of blood ran down the side of my neck. Black spots dancing in my vision, I wracked my brain for anything I could say to save myself.

"An answer," I croaked.

"What was that, dearie?" Zipporah asked with false concern.

When she eased the pressure on my chest, I blurted, "Any question you ask of me, if I know the answer, I'll give it to you."

The harpy straightened and cocked her head this way and that as she considered my offer. "I accept."

She stepped off my chest, and I sucked in a deep breath, undeterred by the atrocious aroma. She crowded close, preventing me from standing, but I was too busy reacquainting myself with oxygen to care.

"I will take my answer another time, Kylie Grayson. You will be in my debt."

Dread sank into my bones. At some point in my future, this vile bird-woman would ask me to reveal a secret, any secret—the name and locations of the gargoyles, the identity of a protected informant, some personal detail that she could use against me—and I would be compelled to give it. I had promised her too much, but I'd had nothing smaller with which to bargain. Zipporah knew she had gotten the better part of our deal, too, and her cackle echoed in the cavern.

She sidestepped to peruse a shelf, and I struggled to my feet in time to see Grant storm into the cavern.

"Don't worry, Grant Monaghan. Your reporter is unharmed," Zipporah said without glancing in his direction.

Grant stopped, but he didn't turn back to cleaning the nest until I waved him off. I wouldn't have called myself *unharmed*, but it was too late for his assistance. I had already made a deal with the harpy.

I brushed the stinging hollow of my throat, and my fingers came away bloody. The cut wasn't much deeper than the scratches her wings had made on the back of my neck. None were life-threatening, but I worried about infection. Even so, I didn't dare use my magic on a self-cleaning spell while in the harpy's den; I couldn't predict her reaction, and I certainly wasn't going to ask for her permission.

Zipporah shifted items on the shelves, using articulating claws that protruded from the bend of her wing. Hardly longer than my fingers, the skeletal digits forced her to wriggle and flap her wings as she rummaged through her treasures. I tugged my shirt over my nose and panted through my mouth.

"Ah, here it is." She stooped to collect the dragon's breath, her bulky body preventing me from getting a look at it. When she straightened, she tucked her mutant fingers and the spriggan weapon out of sight, folding her wings against her body.

I turned to leave, but she slashed the blade of her wing in front of me, thwarting my escape.

"You'll wait here, child." She crowded into the tunnel in front of me and hunkered down, eyes tracking Grant outside in the nest.

I sidled to the wall, as far away from her as I could get, and silently urged the captain to work faster. We couldn't get off this mountain soon enough, and not just because the dryads were depending on us to deliver the dragon's breath. I was beginning to forget what clean air tasted like.

Grant worked methodically, only looking up every few minutes to check on me. His exertions pulled the fabric of his uniform tight across his broad shoulders and defined his thick arm muscles when he added brute strength to his elemental endeavors. Zipporah observed him, unblinking, a repulsive leer contorting her sharp features.

"Mmm, I love it when men strut to impress me," she murmured, as if Grant were putting on a show for her benefit.

I shuddered and hugged my arms around my body.

It took Grant more than an hour to clean the nest, and when he heaved the last of the filth over the side, the woven wooden bowl dipped twice as deep as before. Though he had completed the task far faster than I had predicted possible, impatience wrapped tight around my already tense nerves. The spriggan could have destroyed acres of forest while Grant labored, and it would destroy even more before we reached it. Grant must have felt the same urgency, even if he didn't show it. If there truly had been another way to kill the spriggan, as he had bluffed earlier, he would have taken it.

Grant marched back into the cavern before the last of his elemental weaves dissipated, not stopping until he had subtly placed himself between me and Zipporah. She strutted down the tunnel and we followed. Grant curled his fingers around my bicep, his grip gentle but firm, and guided me into the open air and sunlight. I blinked against the harsh light and gulped untainted oxygen. Soundlessly, he urged me along the outer rim of the nest to where we had first climbed up. The moment we had the dragon's breath, nothing would stand between us and our departure.

Zipporah took an obnoxious amount of time examining every crevice and cranny for anything Grant might have missed. Impatience jittered through my body. Knowing the harpy would further tarry if she sensed my eagerness to leave, I suppressed the urge to bounce, but my toes tapped a frenzied pattern inside my shoes.

"I can find no fault," Zipporah announced an interminable ten minutes later. She flared her wing, the creepy claw-hand unfurling from within the sharp feathers to reveal a small pouch no larger than Grant's coin bag and equally lumpy.

I squinted at the tiny object. I'd assumed the dragon's breath name was symbolic, a trumped-up label for a specialized blowtorch or inextinguishable sword. The misshapen pouch could have literally held nothing more than the exhalation of a dragon. I'd never heard of anything like it.

With a deft flick of her sharp digits, Zipporah tossed the pouch to Grant. "Our trade is complete," she announced.

The moment Grant's fingers closed around the pouch, the harpy dug her talons into the nest, spread her wings wide, and flapped, adding air magic to the wind of her wings. A concussive wall of air slammed into us, lifting us from our feet and catapulting us over the drop-off.

We plummeted through empty space, flailing toward the sharp boulders far below.

9

Arms and legs windmilling uselessly, I stretched a solidified plane of air below us, hoping to slow our plunge. I might as well have spread a handkerchief beneath us and expected it to halt our free fall.

Grant thrust a balance of the elements at me, and I instinctively grabbed hold, drawing on his electrifying power. The moment the link stabilized, Grant seized control. Pain seared my mental pathways as he ripped every particle of magic I could hold through the link—and then more.

The sheet beneath us thickened, strengthened, and grew fire-laced turbines on the underside, pushing upward. We slowed, but not enough. The cleared, sunbaked soil rushed toward us. We wouldn't hit the rocks; Zipporah had launched us far enough that we would splatter against the flat ground instead.

Thick veins bulged in Grant's beet-red neck as he strained to extend the sheet of air, curling it down around the edges like a huge umbrella, and I screamed as the elements tore through me.

I don't want to die!

I yearned to squeeze my eyes shut, but terror pried them wide. We'd drifted over the forest, and the blanket of green canopy crystallized into clumps of individual trees, then into a sieve of thick branches, the details of my final resting place clarifying with terrifying speed. Grant altered the magic sheet, thickening it on my side as he loosened his white-knuckle grip on my bicep.

He was going to try to save me at the expense of his own life.

Blindly, I clutched his wrist, my agonized scream morphing into a denial. I opened myself wider to the elements, my vision tunneling as I shoved magic into the link.

Beyond Grant's shoulder, Quinn rocketed around the harpy's mountain, wings blurred as he strained to reach us. The first branches whipped past. He wouldn't make it in time—

Quinn's enhancement burst through me like a thunderclap. Elements exploded from Grant—air and earth encasing us, fire and air fortifying the sheet beneath us, air and water layering into thick cushions on the ground—his weaves so fast they seemed to spring into existence fully formed.

A millisecond later, we smashed into the elemental cushion, fell through it, and crashed into concrete-hard dirt. Stunned, I lay facedown, unsure if I could move, unsure if I was even breathing. Grant had slowed our descent to half our original velocity, but hitting the cushion of air and water had still felt like landing atop a pillow from a two-story drop.

I sucked in a breath, choking on dust. The movement broke through my shock, awakening a cascade of pain down my body. Coughing, I tested my fingers and toes, surprised they all worked. My knee throbbed, protesting the shift of my tendons. My ribs chimed in with pulses of dull twinges.

I reached for my link with Grant, bolting upright when I didn't find it. He lay on his back, eyes wide open, several feet from me.

Oh no.

What had he been thinking with that fatalistic heroism? I tried to recall the shape of the landing cushion, but it had happened too fast. Had he made it large enough for the both of us?

I scrambled across the twig-strewn ground and peered down at Grant uncomprehendingly. He stared up at the canopy, his teeth bared, his body convulsing . . . with laughter?

"Grant?" I croaked.

His dark eyes swiveled to me. Dirt shadowed the crow's-feet bracketing his eyes, accentuating the amber flecks within his brown irises. I'd never noticed quite how long his lashes were before.

The first hiccup of noise escaped past his lips, then another.

"Are you okay?" I asked.

"That wasn't half as peaceful as birds make it look."

I gaped at him. He chuckled harder.

"Did you hit your head?" I asked.

He patted my hand, too overcome with laughter at his own atrocious joke to speak.

My arms gave out, and I fell back to the dirt, relief and a body's worth of aches mingling with disproportionate irritation. Why had I bothered to be worried? The captain was so dense he probably could have survived the drop without any magical assistance.

Closing my eyes, I ran an internal check on my body, gently manipulating my joints and confirming that though nothing was broken, my body would be an unsightly maze of bruises tomorrow.

Quinn coasted to the ground, landing heavily and running the last few feet to crouch between us, sticking his worried face in mine.

"Thank you, Quinn. You saved our lives." I patted his cheek weakly.

Grant snaked a forearm around the gargoyle's neck and pulled him close to plant a kiss on his forehead. Quinn tumbled against the large man, beaming. I rested a hand on his wing, reassuring myself we were all alive and safe.

"I can't believe Zipporah would—" I stopped myself. Tossing us out of her nest fit her reputation. I had known what I was getting myself into when I'd insisted on accompanying Grant—or I had thought I'd known.

My gut squirmed. I'd barely survived my first encounter with Zipporah, and my debt to her ensured this wouldn't be the last time she and I would cross paths.

I pushed upright but remained seated, not yet trusting my legs. Fidgeting with the hem of my shirt, I glanced at Grant, then away, stumbling over my words. "You were right. I should have listened to you and stayed with Quinn. I shouldn't have followed you."

He burst out laughing, and this time his full-bodied mirth burned my ears.

"If that was your version of an apology, it needs work," Grant said when he caught his breath.

I glared at him. I had been going to thank him for saving my life, but the man was smug enough already.

Grant sat up, shifting the half-grown gargoyle with ease.

"So next time you'll trust me when I tell you something is dangerous?"

"I never doubted you." Did he honestly think I'd give him a definitive answer to such a loaded question?

Grant shook his head. He stood, then helped me to my feet. Straightening jarred my bruised ribs and sent sharp pangs through both knees. I tightened my expression, refusing to show my pain. Insufferable or not, Grant had done everything possible to save us; it would be petty to complain about aches when I was alive.

"What did Zipporah extract from you?" he asked.

My gaze bounced to Grant's and away too fast. "Extract? What do you mean?"

"The harpy had you pinned to the floor. She didn't let you live out of the goodness of her shriveled heart."

I didn't want to admit to Grant how badly I had messed up. I had already admitted he had been right to try to forbid me from going with him to see Beldame Zipporah; I didn't need to give him additional leverage to use against me the next time he succumbed to the urge to order me around. Besides, the deal had been made. Confessing my mistake wouldn't change the outcome.

Grant waited, pinning me with his serious captain's eyes, his gaze saying he could see right through me and any possible lie I might try. I wasn't fooled. He might have been the most powerful warrior I had ever met, both in magic and muscle, but even he couldn't read minds.

"A story," I said, holding his gaze. "I offered to write about Zipporah in the *Chronicle*."

"She accepted that?"

"My head's still attached, isn't it?" My pulse pounded in my throat, and I bent to brush off my pants, using the excuse to gracefully break eye contact.

The caked-on crud from Zipporah's cavern had fused with the forest soil, and my hands didn't make a dent. I reached for the elements, prepared to douse myself with a powerful cleaning spell, but the moment I touched air, pain lanced through my skull. Groaning, I released the magic and clutched my head.

"You're going to want to go easy," Grant said, and only his sympathetic tone curtailed my sarcastic comeback. I hadn't known it was possible for my brain to feel tender.

When the agony subsided to a dull pound, I said, "We can't wait; we got the spriggan to— *The dragon's breath!* Did you see where it landed?" I spun in a fast circle, searching the ground for the tiny pouch.

Grant held up his hand, revealing the pouch safe in his palm. I sagged, bracing my hands on my knees, relief robbing me of my voice.

"What happened up there?" Quinn asked.

"We made a deal with Zipporah." Grant tied the dragon's breath to his belt, cinching it tight.

"Why did she try to kill you?"

"Because I'm an idiot and I didn't negotiate safe passage off her mountain," Grant said.

Quinn continued to pester Grant with questions. I had known the gargoyle enjoyed accompanying me on my various investigative outings, but I hadn't realized how much he had picked up. As adroitly as any *Chronicle* reporter, he teased the who, what, why, and how details out of Grant. I listened with pride as I tentatively stretched my magic and body. Maybe Terra Haven would have its first gargoyle journalist soon. The thought made me smile through the pain as I layered water and air together, gradually increasing the power of the weave until it strengthened enough to remove the worst of the excrement from my hair and clothes. When

I finished, I cycled through the elements, testing my limits. The tenderness subsided with gratifying speed.

Grant cleaned himself off with an efficient spell, then had me hold still while he swept the lacerations on my neck with a disinfecting blend of fire, wood, and water. I gritted my teeth against the burn, blinking rapidly so I wouldn't cry.

"Thank you."

"Can you link?" Grant asked.

"Are you going to pull your weight this time?"

He widened his eyes, quirking his lips to expose his dimples in a practiced look of innocence. "I promise," he said with mock gravity.

I didn't worry about impressing Grant this time and gathered only a nominal amount of each element, combining and passing them to him. He accepted my magic so gently I almost didn't feel the link.

"I won't break," I said.

He eased magic through our link, watching my face for a reaction. I huffed.

"I swear. I'm fine." To prove it, I flooded our link with magic.

"No permanent damage?"

I shook my head. His concerned expression, combined with the sensual, powerful energy of his magic swirling through me, teased unrealistic fantasies to life, and I turned away, busying myself with collecting my bag and checking on my camera to distract myself.

Grant built another air platform, pulling magic evenly from both of us, our link enhanced by Quinn. Then the captain placed his hand on the nearest tree and spoke in a loud voice. "We need the fastest route to the spriggan."

His words splashed ice on my half-formed fantasies, yanking me back to the present. The boughs above us rustled, then those of the tree next to us. Limbs creaked and birds twittered in alarm as the oaks pulled their branches aside to reveal a clear path south.

Grant stepped onto the platform and held his hand out to me. I climbed up behind him and wrapped my arms around his waist, hoping he couldn't feel the tremor of fear that ghosted my arms. Obtaining the dragon's breath had been the easy part. We still had to stop a homicidal creature more powerful than the three of us combined—and our only weapon looked like a bag of air.

10

I clutched Grant's shirt with sweat-damp palms and double-checked Quinn's location. The gargoyle stayed close, gliding between the unnaturally split canopies. Our close call had scared him as much as it had me, and I was more than happy to have him within shouting—and boosting—range.

"What do you know about spriggans?" Grant asked, his voice a rumble against my chest.

I blinked, the afterimage of Quinn's bright golden body flashing across the back of my eyelids. My trepidation over the upcoming encounter had numbed my brain more than I realized if the captain was the one prompting information from me and not the other way around. I wracked my brain for details about spriggans, coming up with rumors and hearsay but few real facts. My readers would likely have even less knowledge about this rare threat, which meant I'd need to ground today's event with facts about the species as well as historical details. Plus, I'd need every last word of this story to shine with evocative information if I had any hope of winning the trip to the everlasting tree.

The reminder of my objective centered me, giving me something to focus on other than my anxiety. I wondered if that had been Grant's intent.

Nah. I was giving him too much credit.

"Spriggans are fierce and almost impossible to kill," I said. "They have bottomless appetites and eat anything and everything in their path. Until today, I thought the only way to stop them was to ring them in fire until it consumes them."

"That's about right, only less 'bottomless appetite' and more 'pathological impulse to destroy anything living,'" Grant said. "Spriggans are strong, quick to adapt to any combative styles they come up against, and impervious to most weapons."

"Except fire."

"And Landewednack dragon's breath."

The ground rose and fell, the hills becoming more pronounced the farther we traveled. I peered around Grant's shoulder, mesmerized by the unfolding line opening in front of us, the trees perpetually parting to provide us with the most direct route to the spriggan. Craning to view behind us proved equally hypnotic: The massive oaks' branches dropped back into place as we passed in an endless shifting of limbs and leaves, restoring the forest to its normal state. Already, Beldame Zipporah's towering mountain had been swallowed by the forest, and drawing a straight line in any direction seemed a fool's fantasy.

"But why attack here and now? Why was it drawn to this grove?"

"Spriggans are from the British Isles. They are guardians of a dryad forest in southern England."

"Guardians? Then why is this one attacking the dryads here?"

"It was probably drawn to this grove because of the familiar dryad magic, and if it were in its right mind, it would never hurt a dryad, but spriggans go mad when they're away from their homeland for too long. Their minds become warped. Now all of its ferocious potential is being brought to bear on the gentle dryads."

Gentle wasn't the term I'd have used to describe the dryads this morning, but I knew what Grant meant. Any creature, no matter how peaceful their nature, could be driven to violence when their homes and lives were threatened.

Wary of fracturing whatever spell had prompted Grant's uncharacteristic willingness to disclose information, I tried to keep my tone light and my questions direct and simple.

"How did it get across the ocean?"

"It must have gotten into the cargo hold of a trader's ship. More foreign creatures than you'd think slip into the country that way."

"How did it get this far inland?"

"On its own two feet. They can travel great distances."

"But why?"

Grant shrugged, and the muscles of his back shifted against my breasts, reminding me of how intimately we were positioned on the tiny, flying platform. Grant must have had the same realization, because he stiffened and didn't move again. For some reason, that made me smile.

"It could have been lost or looking for a mate," Grant said after an awkward pause. "It wouldn't have been thinking clearly."

"So it didn't set out to attack this grove?"

"No."

Quinn's enhancement cut out, then roared back through the link. We both jerked to check on the gargoyle. His wings flared in alarm, then tucked to his sides, and he dropped like the stone creature he was to the forest floor. He'd spotted the spriggan.

My pulse kicked higher, my body stiffening with a surge of adrenaline.

Grant brought the platform to a stop at the base of a small incline, dissolving the plate of air. We dropped to the ground in unison, the maneuver as coordinated as if we'd done it a dozen times. Reluctantly, I let go of Grant and the illusion of safety I enjoyed while wrapped around his strong body. He dissipated our link as he stepped away from me, and the loss of physical contact timed with the withdrawal of his magic curled into a tight sense of abandonment I couldn't quite shake.

With the high sun beating down on my head and shoulders, I should have been hot, but nerves stole my body's heat. I tucked icy fingers into my armpits and surveyed our surroundings. The trees had closed in around us, and this section of forest looked no different than the acres behind us.

Quinn's stone feet pounded through dried leaves and brittle underbrush in a racket loud enough for three gargoyles as he extricated himself from his impromptu landing spot. I started to shush him before realizing we were in no danger of attracting the spriggan's attention. Without the wind whistling against my ears, the cacophony was impossible to miss. I turned to face the hill, my mind conjuring a horrific scene to go with the crack of breaking trees and heavy earthen rumbles.

"It's huge and it's hurting them!" Quinn said, skidding to a halt next to me and leaning against my leg. He looked to Grant with worshipful eyes. "Help them! Hurry!"

"Stay here," Grant said.

I gave him the incredulous look his order deserved.

"Fine. Stay low." Hunched at the waist, Grant trotted up the hill, crouching lower as he reached the crest. I followed, Quinn on my heels. When Grant stopped, I halted beside him and looked up. My breath caught in my throat.

A tornado could have touched down in the forest and done less damage.

A twisted path of devastation three times as wide as Wicker Road stretched from the base of our hill to the horizon, the soil churned with broken tree carcasses ripped into a jumble of ragged limbs and shredded bark. The shriek and pop of an oak being torn asunder jerked my attention to the towering giant at the center of the carnage. A monstrous mix of voracious dryad and human bloated to giant proportions, the spriggan loomed as tall as the oaks it destroyed. Massive trunk legs supported its—no, *his*—thick torso topped by a shockingly childlike face. Where the rest of his walnut-brown body appeared rough, more bark than flesh, his smooth face and delicate nose might have been described as sweet—if not for his terrifying round eyes that spun in search of his next victim, his mouth agape to expose a thicket of splintery teeth. Thorny vines sprang from his fingertips, growing as they whipped across the battlefield to wrap around a tattered stump. With a yank, he uprooted the decapitated sapling and shoved it into his mouth. Beneath his feet, the soil roiled, revealing glimpses of spiked roots tunneling from his toes outward.

I fumbled for my camera with numb fingers. No matter how clever my prose, I would never be able to describe this scene as evocatively as a picture could show it. Even more important, my readers needed to see the dryads' bravery.

Their fragile bodies didn't even reach the spriggan's knees, and if they'd used a direct assault, it would have been suicide. Instead, the dryads stood at the edges of the pandemonium in groups of four and five, employing Grant's tactical strategies. A blackberry bramble snaked across the demolished clearing, not simply moving but growing. Layers upon layers of refined wood magic supported by traces of earth and water fueled its rapid maturation, the weaves too complex to be created by anyone other than a dryad. It would have taken me a month to dissect the spell and another four to re-create it—if I'd possessed the necessary skills with wood, which I didn't. Yet the dryads built and stretched the elaborate weave so rapidly the bramble slithered forward at a walking pace.

Sneaking up behind the spriggan, the bramble reared high and struck around his knee, wrapping its thorny length down the spriggan's calf.

I primed and lifted my camera, snapping pictures as the spriggan stumbled, his assault on a tree across the clearing cut short. The dryads altered the magic around the bramble, and new shoots blossomed along the vine, half tunneling into the ground, the others twining higher up the spriggan's leg, attempting to root him in place. The enraged giant snapped off his own twenty-foot-long vine fingers at his palm. The severed vines fell limp and new ones sprouted to wrap around the bramble and wrench it from his leg. The blackberry vine whiplashed all the way across the savaged clearing to the base of the bush, throwing branches twice its thickness into the air before snapping off.

The spriggan treated his own flesh with even less care, tearing the bramble from his leg and shoving handfuls of it into his enormous mouth. He devoured the thorny plant while his gaze darted around the clearing, locking on to a tree far to our left. On the fringes of the destruction, the oak stood like a jewel, tipped with a lush canopy several feet taller than the surrounding trees. Its health and size suggested it might be a bonded tree, one linked to the life of a dryad just as the dryad's life was linked to it. The two dryad warriors crouched at its base confirmed it. They looked like children, their spindly weapons insignificant against the might of the colossal spriggan.

Deep furrows shot from the spriggan's feet toward the bonded oak, spraying soil and broken limbs in parallel lines. Simultaneously, long vines burst from his hands to wrap around the closest branches of the oak. The spriggan didn't have to move to reach sixty feet away.

"It's going to kill them!" Quinn squeaked.

"We've got to do something." I spun to Grant, wrapping my hand around his thick forearm.

"Look." He pointed across the ravaged ground to a dozen more blackberry brambles snaking toward the giant. Before the spriggan's underground attack could reach the oak, three brambles wrapped around his legs, toppling him. The oak branches in the spriggan's grasp broke free with sharp snaps, leaving the tree mostly unharmed. The spriggan wasted no time tearing at the brambles imprisoning him.

"He won't stay down for long, but they've worked out how to distract him," Grant said.

I nodded, studying the battleground with better understanding. Remnants of blackberry brambles littered the broken ground beneath the hill where we crouched, their lines bright green against the mud- and wood-churned soil. Many more broken ropes of brambles crisscrossed the spriggan's cataclysmic wake, clumped where the dryads had successfully diverted the spriggan from bonded trees.

"Nathan is here." Quinn used a paw to point.

The senior writer huddled well back from the fighting, on another rise where he had a similar height advantage as us. Like me, he had his camera in hand, and the shimmer of a communication capsule beside him captured his voice as he recorded the details for his story. For *my* story.

I snapped my camera shut and stuffed it back in my bag. I'd gotten the pictures I needed; continuing to photograph the horrific events seemed macabre, as if I would be hoping for a more gruesome event to top the already shocking pictures I'd captured.

"Where's your squad?" I asked, surveying the outer perimeter of the destruction.

"On their way." Grant gestured for us to follow him down the hill, away from the spriggan, where we wouldn't be visible to the giant. When we halted, he gripped my shoulders, his heavy hands weighting me down as if he wished he could root me in place.

"Will you remain right here if I order you to?"

I bit my lip.

"You have no business going up against a spriggan," he pressed.

No, I didn't.

Grant seized on my visible indecision. "You're a journalist, Kylie. You need to remain objective, outside of the story, so you can see the whole picture. You can't stick yourself into your own stories and expect to get a well-rounded article."

"That was . . . refreshingly logical, Captain." His words might have come from the editor herself, and he was right. I wasn't a warrior. I didn't have the right personality or skill set. Instead, I'd decided to better the world by protecting people with knowledge, writing articles so everyone could be better informed.

But sitting on the sidelines, crafting an article and hoping I'd win the challenge with it while the dryads fought to save their trees and their lives didn't sit right with my conscience. Nor did sending Grant in alone, not when I could be of assistance.

Nothing says I can't write a more intimate piece, one from the front lines of the battle.

I scoffed at the thought, reading my own attempt to bolster my bravery by giving it a journalistic bent. In truth, I actually thought I could make a difference in this fight. I hoped I wasn't fooling myself.

"We'll be stronger linked," I said.

Grant's face darkened, his expression turning mutinous. I hurried on before he could argue.

"At least until your squad gets here. You'll need—" I started to say he'd need me, but I remembered that humiliating lesson from the climb up Beldame Zipporah's mountain. "You can *use* me, use my magic. You're not exactly your most energized self, Captain Monaghan."

"I'll help, too." Quinn stood tall, though his eyebrows drew together with worry. I patted his neck, proud of his courage.

Grant look back and forth between us, clearly wanting to say yes to Quinn and no to me.

"I won't be left behind." The firmness of my voice surprised me, considering how badly my insides were quaking.

Grant's molars ground audibly. "Fine. Link up. And, Kylie, don't make me regret this."

11

When I stuffed my camera back in my bag, pain sliced into my fingertip. I yanked my hand out and examined the line of blood oozing to the surface, then peered inside my bag. The harpy's metallic feather had fallen free of the protective sheath of my journal. Shaking my stinging finger, I scowled at the feather. I'd completely forgotten I'd put it in there, but seeing it spawned an idea.

Gingerly removing it, I laid the feather on the ground, then packed mud around the needle-sharp quill. When I had a solid pommel of pressed dirt, I encased it in a net of earth and wood and tied off the spell to hold it together. Despite having never made anything like it before, the entire spell had been effortless, thanks to my access to both Grant's magic and Quinn's enhancement. Even so, I sensed the weariness edging our link. We'd been through a lot today, and it had taken its toll on all our energy.

I swung the feather experimentally, listening to the whine of displaced air. Grant would require every drop of our combined magic in his assault, leaving none for me to defend myself. At least now I had a weapon that stood a chance of fending off the spriggan's spiky vine fingers. When I glanced up at Grant, he nodded approvingly.

"I have two rules," Grant said, holding up his fingers as he ticked them off. "Kylie, you get no farther from me than my shadow. Quinn, the opposite goes for you. I want you as far from the spriggan as possible while still boosting us. You've seen his reach; keep your distance. Is that clear?"

Quinn and I nodded. With the sun barely past its zenith, I'd have to stand practically on top of Grant if I were to take his instructions literally.

"Can you boost the dryads, too?" Grant asked.

"I'm already enhancing those I can reach."

"We're lucky to have you with us. Now get to safety." Grant clapped Quinn on the rump, urging the gargoyle into action.

Quinn spun and ran down the hill away from the spriggan, his lope transitioning seamlessly into flight when he spread his wings. In a few hard beats, he surpassed the canopy and circled wide around us.

Grant shifted, pulling my gaze to his. "If we do this right, we're going to draw the spriggan's full wrath. Once we've engaged him, I won't be able to extricate you from the field. No one would think less of you if you remained behind."

I shook my head. "I'm coming," I croaked, my throat parchment dry.

He searched my eyes, his gaze flicking to my white-knuckle grip on the feather. "Leave the bag," he ordered even as he turned to face the spriggan and broke into a jog.

I shrugged free of my bag's strap and dropped it, glancing around to memorize the location. *I will live to return for it,* I promised myself. Then I sprinted to catch up with Grant.

Fear slid a numb hand around my brain, distancing me from my racing pulse and muting the chatter of my panicky thoughts. My feet hit the ground in steady beats, but they might as well have been manipulated by a stranger. Sweat trickled down my back, and I tightened my grip on the feather. All too quickly, we emerged from the dubious protection of the trees on the hill and into plain sight of the spriggan.

"Stay close," Grant said, as if he couldn't resist one final admonishment.

Twigs crackled underfoot; then we reached the larger branches strewn across the ground, and footing became more precarious. We charged over a broken oak trunk, and I thought for sure the spriggan would turn on us, but he remained focused on a tree behind him, oblivious to our approach. Running across the uneven ground on the same level as the spriggan, I lost all sense of perspective. The giant towered as tall as the heavens, and I felt as minuscule as an ant.

Why had I volunteered to throw myself into the path of this deadly creature? Every step closer to the spriggan increased the clangor of my instincts screaming for me to turn around and flee. Grant hadn't hesitated and hadn't looked my direction once. His entire focus remained rooted on the spriggan. Why hadn't I asked him about his battle plan before racing after him?

We cleared a second downed tree, and Grant hurtled a wagon wheel–size fireball at the spriggan to get his attention.

It worked. The spriggan whipped around, mouth gaped wide in a cavernous roar. Snapping off the vines currently entangled in an uprooted bush, he grew new spiked appendages and flung them toward us as fast as if they had been shot from bows. Grant didn't slow, and only my fear of being separated from him kept my legs in motion.

Launching whirling, razor-sharp blades of air to meet the wicked vines, Grant severed all but three before they reached us. I darted forward, slicing the feather-blade through the remaining vines as they spun around Grant's raised arm. Sticky green sap sprayed my face, and the sundered tips of the vines flopped to the ground, but the live lengths grew to replace what I'd cut. I slashed again, evading their grasp; then all three vines fell inert when Grant hacked them off closer to the spriggan. The captain's fist latched on to my pants' waistband, propelling me forward when I would have stopped to catch my breath and reassure myself I was still alive.

As abruptly as the spriggan had focused on us, he turned away, distracted by some other perceived threat. My relief constricted to dismay; his wrath had fallen on a bonded tree. We zigzagged through a snarl of felled oaks and limbs, emerging scratched and alarmingly close to the spriggan. Grant chucked another fireball. The spriggan deflected it with a wall of dirt-encrusted roots. He snapped off the repulsive toelike appendages and immediately tunneled new roots through the soil toward us. The wall remained standing.

Cursing, Grant yanked magic through me, creating lightning out of thin air and exploding it across the ground between us and the spriggan, breaking up the dirt barrier. Splintered wood flew in concussive arcs, and we sprinted through air smelling of charged ozone and charred wood. Grant's impressive bolts of electricity pounded a line straight to the spriggan but stopped before hitting him. Did the spriggan have a defense I couldn't see?

"Get down!" Grant shoved me and I collapsed to my

knees on a tangle of broken limbs. The pop of a snapped whip broke against my eardrum and a thorny vine whistled through the air above me. The tip of it spun, slashing at Grant's back. He countered with shears of fire element, severing the vine before it could land a second blow.

The next vine struck from the opposite direction, the third from straight above, every attack focused on Grant. He countered each strike while spinning a dozen elemental blades through the vine-choked air, severing the thorny tentacles as fast as the spriggan formed them. Awe broke through my terror. Grant wasn't merely holding twice as many elemental weaves as I could; he also manipulated each of them individually and accurately. If I hadn't seen it with my own eyes, felt his magic through the link, I would have said it was impossible.

A surge of spiked roots burst from the ground and tangled around my legs, curling into constricting vises. I sawed the feather against them, but the metal hairs caught in the sap, slowing me. The spikes pulsed, squeezed, and pierced my calves. I whimpered, instinctively scrambling for the elements and crashing against Grant's iron control of our linked magic. He grunted at my unexpected assault, jerking in my direction. The spriggan took advantage of his distraction, angling a vine to strangle him.

Before my warning left my lips, Grant deflected the attack, simultaneously forming two machete wedges out of fire-limed air and hacking into the base of the roots binding me. His blow sank halfway through them and dissipated, leaving me entangled but the spriggan's hold weakened. I sawed the feather into the cuts he'd made, liberating myself as Grant refocused on the snarl of vines. Tripping free of the roots, I regained my feet.

"My foot," Grant barked.

I dropped forward and sawed through a root tangled around his boot, earning a quick "thanks" before he yanked me to my feet and tugged me into a sprint again.

Grant had warned about the spriggan's adaptive fighting style, but I had underestimated how dangerous that made the giant. The first fireball had caught him off guard. The second, he'd been prepared for, and we'd nearly gotten caught. Even if Grant had endless variations of attacks to throw at the spriggan, fatigue whittled away his dexterity—I could feel it through the link. We needed to end this fight fast.

Grant drove magic into the dirt around the spriggan's feet and shoved. The world went fuzzy around the edges, and I fought to keep my footing, energy siphoning from my muscles to counter the magical drain. The amount of power Grant wielded staggered me; even if he'd handed over control of the link, I never would have been able to manipulate the elements in those quantities, at least not with any skill. And he did it while running.

Clawing an extra boost of magic from our link, Grant tunneled into the ground beneath the spriggan. Thick clay soil parted and buried the spriggan to his knees. Grant seized my forearm and ran full out along the path he partially cleared with his lightning strikes. Fifty feet separated us from the spriggan. Thirty. Twenty-five. My heart knocked against my ribs.

Don't trip. Don't trip.

A wall of roots burst from the ground in front of us. We dodged left, but the spriggan anticipated our move. In an explosion of dirt and splinters, the ground erupted around us, not attacking but imprisoning us in a thorny cage. The roots tightened above our heads, blocking out the sun. Grant twirled razor-thin bands of air around our enclosure, hacking and slashing through the barbed trap. I added my own paltry efforts, cutting into the nearest roots with the harpy feather. Small white flowers burst open along the walls of our prison in a rush of sweet perfume, releasing a fine mist of pollen. Pain lanced between my eyes and my vision doubled.

Poison.

I backpedaled into Grant, scrambling for magic through our link. Grant released it to me, and I enveloped our heads in a bubble of fresh air. My vision cleared.

"Poison?" Grant asked, his voice rough with exertion. Blood ran from a cut on his neck and cheek, mixing with sweat and dirt into a gritty slurry that stained the gray collar of his uniform.

Panting, I nodded.

Redoubling his attack on the roots, Grant concentrated on a single exit point, but for every wooden stalk he severed, two took its place. Constrained by the air bubble, I remained pressed to Grant's side, unable to assist. Thick veins corded either side of his neck as he unleashed a flurry of elemental strikes against the base of the roots. A slender section collapsed, revealing a second wall behind the first. We would run out of oxygen before Grant cut through all the layers.

"Fire?" I asked.

"Fire," he agreed.

The draw of his magic through me changed, shifting from the familiar textures of air into the more volatile blends of fire. Dropping a fully formed ring of fire around us, Grant ignited the roots on all sides. He bubbled a second ring inside of the first, this one a shield of water to protect us from the heat, and together we kicked smoldering limbs from beneath our feet.

Instead of retracting, the roots turned rigid. Flames leapt up their side, slowly burning through the wooden fibers.

"He cut off his own root toes and left us in here to burn, didn't he?" I asked.

"Most likely."

I used my grubby shirt to wipe sweat from my face. "Why haven't you set the spriggan on fire?"

"It's too dangerous. If he ran, he'd start a forest fire. Besides, he's sick, not evil."

The spriggan seemed plenty evil to me. Yet, despite our direct charge to the spriggan, Grant's attacks had been measured, and his words triggered my suspicion. Grant had treated the monstrous creature as if—

"You're trying to save him?!"

"With luck."

A blade of a root stabbed through the soil inside our protective water shield, the barbed tip sharp as a spear, the length lined with deadly rows of spikes. Grant slashed it off at the ground, then poured a stream of fire down the hole in the dirt after it.

Our prison walls blackened and crackled under the heat of the flames, and when Grant punched outward with our shield of water, they collapsed, freeing us in a cloud of ash and smoke.

The spriggan had used the time to his advantage, freeing himself from his dirt trap only to be caught in a tangle of brambles directed by the dryads. The spriggan threw back his head in a hollow roar, then lashed out at the dryads, sending small bodies flying. Grant roared right back, funneling all his energy into a barrage of coconut-sized fire-balls, redirecting the spriggan's attention to us.

A straggler root speared up from the ground behind us, and I slowed to sever it before it could tangle in our feet.

"Kylie, where are you?" Grant barked without turning from his assault on the spriggan.

I grabbed his belt with my right hand and staggered backward beside him, using my dominant hand to deflect wayward roots with the dulling edge of the feather.

"What exactly is Landewednack dragon's breath?" It wasn't the time for questions, but I wasn't going to get a better opportunity.

"Dirt."

"Dirt! We almost died getting *dirt*?"

"Dirt from the southern tip of the British Isles." Exertion strained Grant's voice. "From the spriggan's homeland, a special blend of serpentinite, coal, and sandstone."

"But it's called dragon's breath because it'll sear the flesh from that monster's bones, right?" Please let it be that powerful.

"It's called dragon's breath because earth elementals have a twisted sense of humor. But if we can get the dirt on the spriggan, there's a chance it'll restore his sanity."

"A chance?"

A poisonous root shot from the ground between our feet, flowers popping open to release their toxin. I commandeered a trickle of magic and dispersed the lethal pollen as I chopped the vine off at the ground. As soon as we were safe, I relinquished the magic back to Grant for his attack.

"There's a much larger chance he'll kill us first," I said.

Grant spared me a glance, his fierce amber-flecked eyes momentarily arresting me. "I won't destroy a creature just because it's safer or more convenient for me. Not so long as there's a chance of saving it."

The conviction in his tone chased a shiver down my spine, and I filed the statement away to use in my article. That was exactly the sort of sentiment that made Grant a stellar FPD captain, and it was why I couldn't shake this inconvenient crush I had on him.

The soil behind us fell inert, the tiny quivers and churned dirt that indicated an underground assault ceasing. I spun to face the spriggan, bracing myself for a new form of attack. Circular black-edged burns peppered his torso, and mindless rage contorted his youthful face. Sprouting new vine hands, the spriggan clutched the thick trunks of downed trees and flung them with horrifying ease—straight for us.

Grant snatched my hand in his and sprinted toward the monstrous creature. My arm snapped in my shoulder socket and I lurched after him. A fifty-year-old oak sailed through the air on a perfect trajectory to crush us. Grant didn't attempt to deflect it; instead, he added a boost of air to its flight, using the tree's momentum to propel it over our heads. It'd barely cleared us before Grant wrenched magic through the link to alter the aerial path of an enormous root ball. The captain's magic exhibited no finesse; he didn't have the strength to play catch with tree trunks or to counter the spriggan's attacks, only to keep us alive.

For my part, I ran. Staying upright across the rubble-strewn ground while ducking deadly wooden projectiles and attempting to anticipate directional changes took all my concentration. I caught glimpses of the dryads at the edges of the forest, out of range of the spriggan, their foreign wooden faces locked in concentration. Though I couldn't see any blackberry brambles angling for the spriggan, I trusted they were out there. I spotted Quinn once, a second, golden sun in the sky gliding dangerously close. But mostly the spriggan filled my vision—perilous, immediate, and terrifying.

A tangle of vines swooped from the left, wrapping

around Grant's torso and yanking him sideways, almost out of my grasp.

"Grant!" I screamed.

He released my hand, shaking free of my clutching grasp. A flurry of elemental blades diced the vines holding him, but they formed slower than before and more clumsily. His slashes no longer cut all the way through a vine in one sweep, and I couldn't tell if fatigue impeded him or if the spriggan had learned how to combat this attack, too.

The spriggan lifted him, and I lunged for Grant. I caught hold of his belt and clung, both of us suspended several feet above the ground. Vines lashed my arms, and I buried my face against Grant's leg. I'd lost the harpy feather. All I could do was hang on.

"Let go!" Grant yelled. "Kylie, let go!"

I didn't know if he meant me or the spriggan until he said my name. Desperation had taken control of my body, and I shook my head wildly.

The spriggan stole the decision from me, ripping me from Grant with a casual swat of a steely vine. I fell, my scream cut short when the ground knocked the wind from me. I'd fallen little more than five feet, and I'd landed on relatively smooth ground—two miracles my brain processed in the background while I watched the spriggan soar Grant through the air, prepared to fling him to his death.

Grant changed tactics, making a cleaver out of fire and searing straight through the band of vines holding him. He dropped, landing in a crouch far across the torn-up field from me. I sucked in a shallow breath, releasing it with a whimper of relief. Using muscles sluggish from shock and pain, I rolled to a crouch to search for the feather, only then realizing my hands were already full.

I held the dragon's breath.

My heart plunged into my stomach.

Grant patted his belt, then searched the ground around him, tossing twigs and limbs aside. The dismay on his face made it clear he thought he'd lost the dragon's breath in the wreckage of the battlefield.

I waved the pouch above my head and shouted, "I have it!" but the spriggan's roar drowned me out.

"Stay there!" Grant's booming command probably could have been heard in Terra Haven. He sprinted for me, but a fist of vines brought him up short. He evaded the punch, then cut his way free of another vine before the spriggan could fling him farther away. Grant fought relentlessly, but our shared link gave me insight into how much each new weave cost him. He wouldn't be able to cross the distance between us, not while fending off the spriggan's assault, and not with energy left to reach the spriggan alive afterward. Nor did we have time for me to sneak across the field of destruction to deliver the dragon's breath back to Grant.

I cowered in my hiding spot, knowing what I needed to do but too scared to move.

Magic pulled through me hard enough to distort gravity, and I braced a hand beside my hip to stay upright. A surge of fire shot from Grant up the long vines feeding back to the spriggan. Simultaneously, a foul blend of wood, earth, and water tunneled into the spriggan's feet at the base of his roots, rotting the long toes as they formed. Dismay cinched my chest, constricting my lungs; Grant was giving up on saving the spriggan.

I can't let him.

The thought fractured my paralyzing fear. Grant had gone to Beldame Zipporah, bartered with her, and nearly died, all on the chance of saving the spriggan. This entire battle had been as much about protecting the violent giant as defeating him. Seeing a monster, any other person would have killed the spriggan by the fastest means, but Grant saw a creature in need of protection and help—even if, in his current state, the spriggan would happily decapitate him.

If I remained hidden and let Grant kill the spriggan, I'd never be able to look him in the eye again. I'd never be able to look *myself* in the eye again.

I wrapped my fist around the pouch and rose to a crouch, my pulse pounding in my throat. I wasn't going to get a better shot. Grant had the spriggan's full attention.

I charged the giant.

12

I tucked my head down, my entire body curled in anticipation of being swatted flat by the spriggan's massive hand, and ran faster than I'd ever run in my life.

Grant roared a single word: "Kylie!"

Through the link, I sensed fireballs forming as fast as they blossomed against the spriggan's legs, arms, and chest. Grant was attempting to keep him distracted.

I leapt downed trees, crashing through smaller branches. They scratched and clawed at me, but I didn't feel them. I barely even saw them. My world narrowed to the spriggan and the distance between us. For a few glorious seconds, I thought I would reach him before he spotted me. I was close enough to map the stretch marks carved up and down his massive trunk legs, to see the flex and stretch of the distended tendons in his calves, to smell the incongruous clean, evergreen scent of the giant. When fresh green tentacles sprouted from his hands, the crackle and pop drowned out my footsteps, and when his arm whistled through the air above me, vines whipping toward Grant, the back draft buffeted me.

Just a few more steps. Keep watching Grant, you big, scary—

A massive, dirt-clotted root surged from the ground, seizing my legs. I snapped forward, agony searing up the backs of my thighs as my momentum propelled me into an unnatural flex. Kicking and clawing, I scrabbled to free myself, but the spriggan's thorny roots spiraled tighter up my thighs and constricted, ruthlessly grinding my leg bones together. I screamed in pain, and the spriggan's head whipped toward me.

Without taking his gaze from me, he swung a back-handed blow into Grant, using vines thicker than my thighs to sweep the captain off his feet. I struggled harder, fighting the roots binding me, but it was like trying to escape hardened concrete.

His body blocking out the sun, the spriggan bent to examine me, and terror locked my muscles. Enormous round eyes regarded me, hunger burning in their insane depths. The spriggan's creepy, childlike face pushed closer, filling my vision. He smiled, revealing a cluster of jagged wooden teeth longer than my legs. I trembled. His mouth opened wide, wider—wide enough to swallow me whole.

With fumbling fingers, I yanked open the top of the dragon's breath pouch and threw the contents and bag down the spriggan's throat. He reared back, shrieking, the sound drilling through my eardrums. The roots shackling me loosened, and I fell from his grasp, my numb legs refusing to support me. Whimpering, I dug my fingers into fistfuls of shredded wood and brambles, straining to drag my sluggish body away from the spriggan. Flailing vines hooked my side, tossing me several feet and slamming me against a broken stump. Head reeling, I yanked magic to me and built a shield of air to encase myself, but the spriggan crashed a fist of vines through it, catapulting me across broken limbs like a ragdoll. Moaning, I curled into a fetal position, my entire body throbbing.

A golden meteor crashed to the ground beside me, then enveloped me in stone wings. Quinn pressed us both to the ground, his head tucked against me beneath his wings, and I curled around his hunched body, hugging him to me. A complex air shield formed over us, and I clutched it, sobbing with relief as I took control of Grant's weave and cocooned Quinn and myself in time to deflect the spriggan's next slap. I had the impression of blades of air and fire through the link, but then the giant roared and battered us, the blows scraping us back and forth across the jagged ground. Quinn dug his claws into the earth, and I clung to his neck for all I was worth, fighting to hold the shield.

When the assault slackened, then ceased, I didn't trust it. Quinn kept his head tucked beneath his wings, his cool quartz breath gusting across my neck. A maelstrom of crunching exploded nearby, and Quinn and I squeezed even tighter together. Then it quieted to an eerie creaking whine, and when that faded, the only sounds left were human-size footsteps cracking through the rubble.

"You guys can relax now," Grant said.

Quinn whiffled against my neck one last time before popping his head out above his wings. A moment later, he folded his stone feathers against his side, allowing me to stand.

I rose stiffly, sharp needles of pain replacing the numbness in my legs. Quinn propped me up, and I leaned heavily on the gargoyle, looking first to Grant to assure myself he was intact, then searching the rubble for the spriggan's massive body.

It had disappeared.

Oh no. "Did you have to kill him? Where's the body? Did you incinerate him?" No, not even the captain could have created a fire hot enough to burn a creature the spriggan's size to ash that quickly. I jerked to take in our surroundings. "Did you bury him? Did he run—"

"Take a breath, Kylie," Grant said.

"Are we—"

"A breath. Now."

I dutifully sucked in air.

"Come here," he said, adding, "Quietly," when I opened my mouth to demand an answer.

I limped after Grant as he tramped through the most heavily churned soil at the center of the destruction. There, in the midst of the wrecked trees, lay a small being no larger than a toddler with the dark wood skin of a dryad and the impish triangular face of a boy. Eyes closed, his sides slowly expanded and contracted. He was asleep.

"The spriggan shrank," I said, feeling the need to state the obvious.

"This is his normal size." Grant circled the spriggan, using gentle weaves of wood and water to assess his health. "Spriggans only swell up like that when they're threatened. Or their dryads are."

"Or when they go crazy," I said.

Quinn crept forward, sniffing the air around the tiny spriggan, the action more catlike than gargoyle. "Are you sure it's safe? He won't attack anymore?"

"The dragon's breath bought us a few days, and I'll make sure he's safely home before he wakes."

Grant stripped off his shirt. The move was so unexpected, I simply stared at his broad, sun-kissed chest. His abdomen flexed as he tugged his shirt over his shoulders, revealing sculpted biceps and muscled forearms to match the rest of him. A dozen scratches crisscrossed his torso, none deep. The protective spells in his clothing had spared him worse injury.

My fingers itched for my camera, my hand actually fumbling in the air beside my hip before I remembered my camera and bag lay on the other side of the battlefield. I also realized I was standing flat-footed, staring at Grant like I never seen a perfect male chest before. Thankfully, he was too busy creating a sling out of his shirt to notice me gawking. I allowed my gaze to linger on his back as he bent to scoop the tiny spriggan into the cradle of his shirt, but I forced myself to look away before he straightened.

When I turned aside, pain jabbed my foot. A twig protruded from the shredded leather of my shoe. More detritus clung to the tattered hem of my pants. The only protective spells in my clothing were the kind that countered wrinkles, and I had more than my fair share of cuts beneath them. Most were on my arms, and I peeled back my sleeves to make sure none needed immediate attention. They stung but, for the most part, were shallow. I lifted my shirt to examine my stomach, poking gingerly at a tender spot over my ribs.

"Are you hurt?"

Grant's gaze slid over my bare midriff, then down my legs and back up my chest. I fought a blush. *He's looking for wounds, not checking me out.*

"I'm just scratched. It's nothing serious." I dropped the hem of my shirt. I knew without looking that my knees would be black and blue and tender for a while after the squeeze a spriggan had given them, but it wasn't worth mentioning. When my gaze fell on Quinn, I forgot about my own injuries. Gouges sliced through his citrine body like malicious carvings. I rushed to his side.

"Oh, Quinn! Look at you! We'll get you straight to Mika when we reach Terra Haven."

Quinn left off nosing a particularly deep cut on his forearm and raised his chin. "I'm just scratched. It's nothing serious," he said, copying my words and tone exactly.

Grant snorted. I shot a glare in his direction before turning back to the young gargoyle.

"You saved my life twice today, Quinn. Thank you. I couldn't have asked for a braver companion."

He wriggled closer to me, eyebrows drawn. "I thought you were going to die. It scared me."

I smiled. "It scared me, too."

"Promise me you'll stick to reporting from the sidelines in the future," Grant said, regarding me with his granite-hard captain's expression. My spine stiffened, an argument poised on the tip of my tongue, until I read the concern in his eyes.

"I'll do my best," I said.

Grant sighed.

Movement at the periphery of my vision pulled my head around in time to witness the last of the dryads circling the destruction and melting into the forest in the direction of Colden Creek. I looked for Potentate Heartwood in their numbers but didn't spot her. Rubbing tingling fingertips against my jeans, I stared after the dryads.

The forest lay hushed around us, seemingly empty of all life but the three of us and the unconscious spriggan. I remembered the frightened coyotes and panicked oxen. We likely *were* the only creatures in Emerald Crown Grove right now.

The drone of a familiar male voice drifted across the

field. I gritted my teeth and amended the thought: just the spriggan, the three of us who stopped him . . . and Nathan.

The senior writer crept closer now that the battle was over, the useless jerk. Where had he been when Grant was being flung through the air? Where had he been while the spriggan was doing his best to kill me and Quinn? If Nathan had linked his magic to ours, we would have been that much stronger. But, no, he'd stood on the fringes and observed.

I couldn't catch the specifics of his words—those fed directly into the communication bubble floating against his chest to be stored for later use—but I knew the gist. He was stealing my story. The bastard.

"Where's the rest of your squad?" I asked Grant. "Shouldn't they have gotten here by now?" I left unsaid that we could have seriously used their help.

"They're probably still dealing with the poisonous river serpent nest that hatched in Lincoln River," Grant said without looking up. "Cleanup is a real pain with those."

Of course. The story I had to beat. How could I have forgotten? Too busy trying not to die, I guess. Even so, I should have put it together sooner. The city guards wouldn't have been equipped to handle the disposal of serpents; a task that dangerous required the special skills of Terra Haven's FPD magic heavyweights.

Grant finished situating the sleeping spriggan in his shirt sling, then draped a loop around his neck so the spriggan rested against his chest. The image momentarily arrested my thoughts—both how good paternal looked on Grant and how chilling it was to see the violent creature snuggled up against his bare chest. If the spriggan woke, it could spear a vine straight through Grant's heart before he could react.

The shutter click of a camera snapped me out of my daze. Nathan stood on a downed tree at the edge of the destruction, lens aimed at Grant and the spriggan.

Then my brain processed the ramifications of Grant's words.

"You knew they were never coming, didn't you?" I hissed the question, projecting my voice too low for Nathan to overhear.

Grant shrugged. "The odds were slim, but at least Nathan got word to my squad so they would know where to come next if I had failed."

His matter-of-fact acceptance of his own possible death left me speechless.

Grant cupped an arm underneath the spriggan, supporting the small creature's weight as he turned to survey the damage. "Good thing we got here so fast. This guy did an incredible amount of damage in just a few hours."

I rubbed my thumb against my tingling fingertips. "You're sure the spriggan showed up only a few hours ago? Not days ago?"

"Definitely only hours." Grant walked the perimeter of the spriggan's former footprint, sending tiny test pentagrams into the ground, checking for who knew what. "This guy has probably been roaming around partially crazed for a while, maybe weeks, but the familiarity of the dryads' forest was likely what triggered his complete loss of control. If he'd gone unchecked for days, the forest would be decimated." He looked up and winked at me as he added, "Not to mention, I'd be terrible at my job."

His words confirmed my suspicions from this morning; I'd been tracking the rumors of restless dryads for weeks. Unless they'd had a collective premonitory vision about the spriggan, something else was going on in Emerald Crown Grove.

"You know he's stealing your story, right?"

I followed Grant's gaze to Nathan, watching as the reporter scurried down a narrow path toward Terra Haven. I visualized the weave to create a fireball, having learned the elemental structure during to my link with Grant, but I dismissed it before it formed, just as I dismissed the impulse to sprint after Nathan. Even if I had the energy to run all the way to Terra Haven, even if I could write the perfect story on the way and type it up faster than Nathan, I couldn't prove the story had been mine first and Nathan was the thief. Dahlia would be more likely to take the word of a senior writer than her newest hire; at best, I'd look like a slacker without the ambition to find my own stories, and at worst like a whiner and a plagiarizer.

I released a heavy sigh, cupping a hand over my ribs when the motion stretched a bruise. "Yeah, I know."

"Do you want me to detain him until you get your story submitted? It's the least I could do."

Grant's offer warmed me to my toes, and I was sorely tempted. "No, but thank you. He can have this story." I managed to say it without grinding my teeth. Almost. "I've got something even better in mind."

I crossed my fingers. I hoped I was right.

13

Q uinn and I parted ways with Grant at dusk, the captain with the spriggan still bundled against his bare chest striding off to book the quickest transport home for the volatile creature, Quinn and I trudging toward the *Chronicle*. When I suggested Quinn go directly home to check in with Mika and get his wounds seen to, he refused.

"You always say the story isn't done until it's turned in. I'm coming with you," he said.

I smiled and didn't try to send him away again.

My own cuts and scrapes had been tended to by Grant, all disinfected and a few of the deeper gouges patched with magic. He'd made me promise to make an appointment with a healer tomorrow, and I fully intended to keep my word.

Around us, Terra Haven was going to bed, all the shop fronts shutting down for the day. A few restaurants remained open, but all carpet rental shops were closed. We caught a late airbus through downtown, Quinn riding on the roof to the delight of the few passengers and the driver.

Rather than fly to his usual perch atop the roof, the gargoyle shuffled up the steps to the *Chronicle* at my side, and I held the door open for him. Exhaustion draped his shoulders, weighing down his head. I had a feeling the moment he stopped moving, he'd pass out. I felt the same way.

At this late hour, only a few reporters hunched over their typewriters in the bullpen, lamps or glowballs illuminating their workstations. Nathan wasn't among them.

I plodded straight to the darkroom, planning to develop my photos first so they would have time to dry while I wrote. Fortunately, my camera and bag had been right where I'd left them, unharmed, and I'd snapped a few pictures of the tiny spriggan strapped to Grant's chest when he wasn't looking—for the *Chronicle*, of course, and in case Dahlia wanted a visual for a follow-up article.

I expected to find the darkroom empty, but Stella puttered inside. The red-tinted glowball turned her thick white braid orange and softened the deep grooves of her face. I hadn't yet learned everyone's names, but Stella and I had bonded during hours of shared time in the miniature lab. As the photography department's head developer, she had been kind enough to teach me a few tricks to get the most out of my pictures, too.

Stella took in my appearance, then Quinn at my side. The red light mixed with his golden tones, casting a stunning rainbow of sunset colors through the gargoyle's thick stone ruff and across his wings.

"Do you need medical help?" Stella asked.

I scanned my clothes self-consciously. I'd gotten strange glances on the bus, too, but mainly people had been more interested in Quinn. My shirt hung in tatters; my pants flaked mud and blood and remnants of the harpy's nest onto the hardwood floor. I knew I must smell awful, but my nose had grown accustomed to my own funk.

"It's not as bad as it looks." I fumbled into my bag for my camera, and Stella surprised me by taking it from my hands.

"I'll develop these, hon. I wouldn't want you to mix up the chemicals in your addled state. And I imagine you've got an important story to write; you got that look in your eye."

"Thank you." Tears misted my vision, my gratitude disproportionate in my exhausted state.

Stella started to pat me on my shoulder, hesitated at touching my filthy garment, and settled for tapping the back of my hand before shooing me from the darkroom.

Someone had left a copy of the evening edition of the *Chronicle* on every typewriter squeezed onto the small table at the junior writers' shared workstation. Not someone; Nathan.

SPRIGGAN ON A WARPATH OF DESTRUCTION. The headline spanned the front page, and a picture of Grant fighting the spriggan wrapped through the fold. The picture had been framed to capture Grant's small figure in juxtaposition with the giant spriggan, and no one would have guessed that if the shot had been shifted an inch to the right, I would have been in the photo, too.

I skimmed the article. Nathan made no mention of me at all. His details on why the dragon's breath worked were conspicuously absent, glossed over in his praise of Terra Haven's illustrious FPD captain. He made no mention whatsoever of where the dragon's breath had come from. Omitting information on Beldame Zipporah had probably been wise; having met the harpy, I had no desire to aggrandize her in any way that might encourage others to seek her help and endanger their lives. The weight of the favor I owed her hung over my head, though it had been well worth it to save the dryads and spriggan—and my own life.

Despite all it lacked, the article still told a stellar story. It grated to see Nathan's name in the byline instead of mine. I wondered if the placement of the newspapers atop my workstation had been to discourage me from writing my own version of the story or simply a means for Nathan to gloat. Probably both.

"I should never have mentioned the dryads in front of Nathan," Quinn said, his wings hunched above his shoulders.

I shook my head. "You're not responsible for the fortitude of his character. Or rather, the feebleness of it. We'll just make sure he never gets the scoop on us again."

"He doesn't deserve the credit. That was your story. You were the one who risked your life." Quinn's tail lashed back and forth, knocking the chair behind him over and drawing the attention of the few other writers in the bullpen.

I rested a soothing hand on his wings, quieting him. "We saved the dryads. And the spriggan. That's what matters."

"Of course, but he stole your story."

"He's shortsighted. He got one big article, but I got fodder for dozens today."

I plopped into a chair, stifling a groan at the simultaneous pangs of pain and relief throughout my body. Grumbling, Quinn lay down beside me. I flipped the newspaper over so I couldn't see the front page, then did the same to all the papers near me before melting against the back of the chair. My brain zinged with the story I'd been mentally crafting over the last couple hours, and I wouldn't be able to fully relax until I got it out.

I open my battered notebook and on the table, then pulled out a string of basic-level communication spells, where I'd captured some of my verbal notes and stored them in tight weaves of air. With my pen poised above my journal, I listened to my recordings, jotting down an outline and making notations in the margins. Then I straightened and started typing.

When I looked up, I was shocked to see the clock hands had swept past midnight. Quinn lay asleep beside me, his massive paws twitching in a dream. The bullpen had emptied, though I hadn't noticed anyone leaving. The only other light in the office came from a crack in the editor's doorway. Sluggish relief pulsed through my weary body. I wouldn't have to wait until morning to submit my article.

I yawned and stretched, cutting the movement short when it elicited a chorus of pain. Bending, I woke Quinn with a soft hand on his back, leaving it there until he oriented on his unfamiliar surroundings. Shouldering my bag, I walked to the editor's office, Quinn padding softly behind me. Sitting cramped over the typewriter for hours hadn't done my body any favors, and I staggered like a newly woken statue, every joint stiff, my coordination clumsy.

Laughter trickled from the editor's office, but it cut off when I knocked on the door.

"Come in," Dahlia said.

I pushed open the door, startled to see the other voice I'd heard belonged to Raquel. I hadn't expected the gryphon rider to be here this late.

Raquel stood, striding from the chair in front of Dahlia's desk to the editor's side to present a united front. "We've been waiting to see what's got you looking like a gryphon cub's chew toy."

I glanced down, once again nonplussed to see the day's events manifested in my dirty, bloody clothes. I must have been more exhausted than I realized if I couldn't keep track of my own body's condition. Flustered, I waved a dismissive hand at my torn outfit. "Oh, this doesn't have anything to do with my story. Not really. This happened earlier today."

"Explain." Dahlia's commanding tone would have done Grant proud.

"You know most of the story. Well, I mean, the stench is from Beldame Zipporah, but the clothing is sort of . . . spriggan tailored." I giggled at my own joke. The bright lights of the office hurt my eyes, and my body radiated too much heat, signaling my eminent crash. I just had to keep it together long enough to submit my story.

Raquel tapped her nose. "Aha! That's definitely the odor of the harpy."

"Nathan mention you tagged along," Dahlia said, "but not the extent to which you . . . participated? . . . in today's events."

"Did someone say my name?" Nathan strode into the office behind me. He'd changed his clothes and showered since the last time I'd seen him, and he looked fresh and competent, everything I wasn't at the moment.

"I thought you'd gone home," Dahlia said.

"I tried, but I was too concerned about Kylie." Nathan stopped halfway between the editor's desk and me, waving a magnanimous hand in my direction. "I enjoy the opportunity to mentor the younger journalists. Kylie was with me today, but . . . I was afraid this might happen. Ky, tell me you didn't also write about today's events. As you saw, I already covered that. Taking you along was just meant to be part of your training."

I longed to punch him and was too tired to keep the unfriendliness from my expression. Aiming for a sweet tone,

I said, "Your lesson today will be *invaluable* in my career." It came out venomous.

Quinn's golden eyes caught the light, and Nathan found an excuse to hurry across the room and take a seat at a small table out of the way. When I turn my attention back to Dahlia, she and Raquel were sharing a glance I couldn't interpret. I swallowed my frustration. If I hadn't been so tired, I never would have allowed Nathan to make me look bad in front of my boss.

"You said you had a story that happened *after* the spriggan battle?" Dahlia asked.

I stepped forward and thrust my typewritten pages into her hand. She didn't turn her attention to them right away, continuing to study me.

"Take a seat before you collapse, Kylie."

I sat in Raquel's vacated chair. Quinn approached the editor's desk and peered over the top. A twinkle of amusement lit Dahlia's eyes as she took in the gargoyle's keen interest; then she started reading. Raquel shifted around to read over Dahlia's shoulder. Nathan twitched, as if he considered taking the same liberty, then thought better of it.

Following my hunch, Grant, Quinn, and I had trekked after the dryads to Colden Creek, then past it to a large beacon of magic stirring in the valley beyond it. We crossed Wicker Road, still free of traffic since Grant hadn't yet removed the warning beacons. We found the dryads ringing a sun-drenched meadow, the normally secretive creatures gathered in the open.

Though we made no attempt to mask our approach, the dryads ignored us. Either our assistance against the spriggan had proved we were trusted allies or Grant's herbal theriaca had earned us more goodwill than I'd understood.

Nevertheless, we stopped short of the meadow, in the shade of a bonded oak.

The dryads had abandoned their weapons, their peaceful demeanors restored. Tranquility suffused their features, and I struggled to recall the creatures who had terrified me less than twelve hours earlier. None stood as tall as my hip, and all looked as if a strong breeze would break them, yet this morning when they'd boxed us in, wooden spears clutched in twiglike fingers, teeth bared, I'd been sure they would kill us.

At first, I noticed only the dryads standing in the meadow, but gradually I spotted more clinging to the limbs and trunks of the nearest trees. Their barklike skin provided impeccable camouflage, and in normal circumstances, people saw a dryad only when a dryad chose to be seen. When I'd learned of two people spotting dryads near Colden Creek a few weeks earlier, my curiosity had been piqued. I'd deployed my rumor scouts and headed to the library to research the reclusive creatures. The conclusion I'd drawn had been exciting, hopeful—and nothing like the violent attack of the spriggan.

I'd crossed my fingers, hope resurging that my original guess had been right.

Intricate wood magic swirled from dryad to dryad, linking those on the ground to those in the trees in a complex elemental net. The magic built, folded in on itself, and expanded in hypnotic waves unlike anything a human congregation could have created. Entranced, I didn't notice Potentate Heartwood until she was several steps into the circle. Trailing filaments of elemental wood, she glided through the short grasses, stopping at the center of the meadow.

When she knelt, the dryads began to chant in their own

foreign language. The soft soughing of their voices skimmed the landscape, reshaping it with the gentleness of a breeze, and the grasses parted around the potentate, revealing rich, dark soil.

A tiny green sprout pushed through the soil in front of her, growing a few inches before unfurling a trio of emerald-green oak leaves. Increasingly intricate magic cycled through the dryads, almost all of it wood, but so many variations and textures that it resembled a tapestry of elements. Quinn sighed with happiness, and I figured he must have been boosting all the dryads, reveling in their extraordinary elemental manipulations even as they benefited from the gargoyle's enhancement.

The potentate hooked the center of the magical tapestry, drawing it to her, and I forgot about Quinn. I forgot to breathe. She spun strands of wood element more delicate than spiders' threads and infinitely stronger, creating a lace-work of magic around the tiny shoot. When she plucked a small shape no bigger than an acorn from her abdomen, a surge of righteous joy filled me; my instincts had been right —the potentate had been pregnant.

Setting her infant on the ground beside the tiny oak, she continued to spin the dryads' daedal magic into a binding spell that would forever connect her child with its tree. Around us, the chanting swelled, then silenced. The magic collapsed inward on the joined infant and seedling, drawing them together until I couldn't see where one stopped and the other began.

Quinn and I leaned forward, mimicking the dryads in the circle, craning to get a look at the newborns. I had primed my camera when we'd first arrived, and I snapped several discreet pictures, silencing the camera's mechanical noises with a buffer of air. Then, at some signal I missed, the dryads surged forward, blocking the babies from sight. Smiling and laughing, they embraced the new mother, and the trees shook their leaves in celebration.

Grant, Quinn, and I had slipped away as quietly as possible. I hadn't been the only one dabbing tears from my eyes, either. Now, standing in the editor's office, I could still conjure the enchantment of that perfect moment of joining, and I'd done my best to project the charm and wonder of it into my story. The joining of a dryad infant and its tree had never been recorded before—not in any records I'd found. Being privy to this rare and beautiful event had been an honor, and I wanted readers of the *Chronicle* to feel the same reverence I'd experienced.

Dahlia set down my pages and didn't protest when Nathan snatched them up. She studied me thoughtfully, then rifled through pictures on her desk. I hadn't seen Stella deliver them, but I recognized my photos. Crossing my fingers beside my legs, I strained to check them out upside down. . . . They were good! I hadn't been sure on the lighting or if my camera had even been functioning correctly, but the baby was clear, and the earlier shots of Potentate Heartwood shrouded in shadows were all the more compelling for the dim lighting, especially those of Grant kneeling in front of the regal dryad.

Raquel picked up a shot of the spriggan, his mouth agape and his leg wrapped in brambles. He filled the left side of the image, and a blur of coiled vines whipped toward fingernail-tall dryads on the edge of the picture. She glanced at my torn outfit again and shook her head, mouthing, "Spriggan tailored."

I tried to smile, but my face had gone stiff while I waited for Dahlia's judgment of my article.

Raquel reached past Dahlia and lifted another photo

from the stack—one of Grant cradling the tiny, sleeping spriggan against his bare chest. It was one of the pictures I'd taken when we'd retrieved my camera, and I'd caught the captain unaware, his attention on the horizon, sunlight glinting in his eyes. The picture could have been a recruitment poster for the FPD: Grant all muscles, his rugged features gritty and abraded from the fight, holding the creature he'd just defeated as tenderly as he might hold his own child.

"Next time female subscription rates drop, here's your front-page picture, Dahlia." Raquel tossed me a wink.

The editor's expression remained unreadable. I took a deep breath and launched into my pitch.

"I was thinking I could do a couple of follow-up pieces on the dryads. The FPD captain would be a great source. He seemed to have a rapport with them. Especially Potentate Heartwood. The articles could be included alongside stories about the cleanup in the grove and maybe I could coordinate with contacts on the coast and the British Isles to report on the spriggan's progress home, and—"

"No," Dahlia cut me off. "You're going to be too busy with the everlasting tree to do all that."

"What?!" Nathan burst from his chair, tossing the pages of my story onto Dahlia's desk. "But that's just a story of a kid being born. How can you say that's better than the spriggan battle?"

Dahlia tapped my pages. "You've done something unique here, Kylie; you've given us a glimpse of an event no one has seen before. Your story captured the style of reporting I want at the everlasting tree—personal and immersive and riveting."

"But there's still time. The contest isn't over," Nathan sputtered.

"Look at this." Dahlia held up the picture of the baby dryad clinging to the fragile stalk of the new oak. The camera hadn't been able to capture the glow of magic around them, but it had caught the wonder and other-earthliness of the moment. "Readers are going to eat this up. Nothing is going to top a baby dryad."

"I'm going?" I asked, not quite believing.

Dahlia nodded.

"I'm going!" I launched from my chair with a shout and shimmied in place. "Thank you! You won't regret this!" I'd done it! I'd won!

"Can I come, too?" Quinn asked me.

"Are you kidding? You earned this as much as I did. Of course you can come!"

The gargoyle danced in place, his antics shaking the floor and rattling the shelves. He immediately stilled, expression contrite, but when he saw Dahlia's and Raquel's amusement, he relaxed.

Nathan stormed from the office, his face red, his fists clenched in anger. I barely noticed his departure.

I couldn't stop grinning. I was going to see an everlasting tree bloom!

"So," Raquel said, cocking a hip against Dahlia's desk, "any idea what you're going to ask the tree?"

DON'T MISS THE SERIES THAT STARTED IT ALL!

To help a baby gargoyle, Mika will risk everything...

 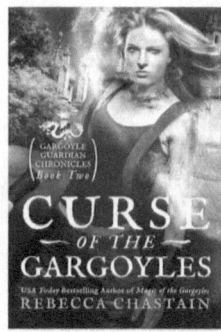 

"unique and captivating right from the start"

-The Reading Diaries

RebeccaChastain.com

Read on for an exciting excerpt from

A FISTFUL OF EVIL

the first in the international bestselling
Madison Fox urban fantasy series by
Rebecca Chastain

AVAILABLE NOW!

Madison's new job would be perfect,
if not for all the creatures trying to
eat her soul…

A FISTFUL OF EVIL

The interview was a catastrophe. It started out fine—better than fine. Kyle, the sales manager for the bumper sticker company Illumination Studios, met me in the warm confines of a nearby Starbucks, purchased me a grande green tea, and selected a table in the corner, away from the door and the cold blast of November air every customer brought in with them. Soft music, cappuccino-machine clacks and whirs, and the murmur of conversation created a cocoon of privacy.

I handed Kyle a copy of my résumé, determined to prove myself to be the mandatory employee for the boring junior sales associate position. I wasn't particularly qualified and I would normally have rather ripped off hangnails than perform cold calls—which is what I strongly suspected the position entailed—but four weeks of unemployment, seven failed interviews, and escalating credit card bills proved very strong motivators.

Strong enough for me to ignore the desperate reason I'd applied for the job in the first place. *Never trust your soulsight,* I told myself for the thousandth time. But my imminent eviction trumped mistrust of my bizarre, mutant vision.

Kyle dropped my résumé to the table without glancing at it. He scrutinized me over the top of his dry cappuccino. Kyle exuded salesman, from his maroon button-up shirt and khaki trousers to his thinning brown hair with its frosted tips. His face was pinched, as if someone had pressed his baby flesh between their hands and pulled, extending his nose and pulling his lips and eyes in tight. He couldn't have been much older than me, despite the sullen brackets around his mouth and deep grooves between his eyebrows. Maybe his expression fell into disapproving lines naturally.

"How many years' experience do you have, Madison?" Kyle asked.

"Specifically in the bumper sticker business, none, but I believe my time at Catchall Advertising will—"

"I don't care about the bumper sticker crap. I care about your experience in the field."

My weirdo radar, dulled by the overpowering mix of desperation and determination, flickered to life.

"I honed my sales skills while working as a saleswoman at Sundage Cars. My experience there taught me how to connect with people from all walks of life." Though it hadn't taught me how to sell a car. In the six months of my employment as a used-car saleswoman, I sold a grand total of zero cars, which is why David Sundage, my cousin-in-law and owner of Sundage Cars, had fired me at the beginning of September. But I wasn't going to concern Kyle with that minor detail.

Kyle set his cappuccino down on the table and leaned back in his chair. "How old are you?" he asked.

"I'm not sure I understand the relevance—"

"What regions have you worked in before this?"

Regions? "I've worked mainly in Roseville since I—"

"With who? Not with Brad or Isabel." Kyle leaned forward, his dark eyes intense.

Who? I eased my tea to the table and ran my palms down the sides of my black knee-length skirt, telling myself it was only nerves that were making Kyle seem so volatile.

"Um, most recently with David Sundage," I said.

"Where are his headquarters?"

Headquarters? What is this, the FBI? Hadn't he bothered to read my résumé?

"Down Douglas," I answered, pointing vaguely west toward Douglas Boulevard and the car lot.

"Before that?"

"Also in Roseville, at Catchall—"

"Look, we can both stop playing this game. I don't care about what jobs you've had to take between IE positions." Kyle deflated into his chair with a gusty sigh. "To be honest, you're the only qualified person to apply for the job—my job. I've been ready to transfer for months now, so I'm not going to make this interview hard on you. I want you to take this job as much as you want it. I just need to make this interview look good so Brad signs my walking papers, okay?"

I nodded and tried to look like I understood more than the English words he used. I didn't know what he meant by "IE positions," and I knew I wasn't qualified for his sales manager position. I wasn't even qualified to be a junior sales associate, but who was I to argue? Managers probably didn't have to make cold calls, which automatically made the job more appealing. Plus, a management position would pay better, and I was pretty sure I could fake it until I got caught up on my bills. By then, I could find a more suitable job. Something more Indiana Jones and less Bridget Jones.

"Okay, let me make this perfectly clear," Kyle continued. "Which wardens have you worked with?"

"Wardens?" As in prison?

Kyle leaned forward, placing his hands on the table. "What's the largest evil you've ever tackled? A wraith? A pissed-off dryad?"

I cast a quick glance around for a candid camera, noting the nearest exit in case I needed to make a run for it. I'd been nervous on interviews before, but never because of a mentally unstable interviewer. Was that why Kyle had insisted we meet away from the company office? Did he even work for Illumination Studios?

I eased my hand through the strap of my purse and slid it onto my shoulder, careful not to make any sudden movements that might spook the deranged man. "I don't think I'm the right person for the job, after all," I said, and pushed away from the table.

This is why I never used my soul-sight, never followed its false leads. I shouldn't have made an exception for this job. To the marrow of my bones, I knew soul-sight was untrustworthy.

"Hang on, Madison," Kyle said, grabbing my arm as I started to stand. I froze. "You're definitely the right person for the job. You're the first enforcer to walk through that door in nearly two weeks."

"I don't even know what that means. I'm going to save us both some time and leave now." I tugged to free my arm.

"Holy crap! You're a rogue." Kyle jerked away from me, shaking his hand like I'd given him cooties. Unbalanced, I fell back into my chair.

"That explains your age," Kyle said, speaking more to himself than me. "And your job history. You haven't been playing games with me . . ."

I stood again as he trailed off, and his gaze snapped to focus on my face. "It was nice to meet you," I said by rote. "Good luck with—"

"One question." Kyle stood, cutting off my escape. He towered over my five-foot-ten frame by a good eight inches. Despite his wiry build, the odds weren't in my favor that I could knock him down before he could grab me.

Taking a deep breath, and reminding myself that I was in a safe public place filled with people, I said, "Okay. One more."

"Did you apply because you thought you could pretend to be qualified for a sales position or because the ad glowed?"

My breath caught. The fact that the job description in the "Help Wanted" section had glowed in soul-sight had been an inexplicable anomaly. Dead, mashed pulp couldn't glow. It wasn't alive. It didn't have a soul. But hearing that Kyle knew about the glow set my arm hairs on end. No one knew about soul-sight except my best friend, and that was only because I'd told her. Soul-sight was my own personal aberration.

Seeing my hesitation, Kyle plowed on.

"Three decades as a rogue has got to be a new record. I'm not sure why you chose to come out of hiding, but I'm not letting you get away now, not when I'm this close"—he pinched his forefinger and thumb together—"to escaping this puny region for some real action."

"I haven't been hiding. I think you're mistaken—"

"Come on. We both know you're not qualified for a sales position even if it did exist," Kyle said, flicking my résumé. The crisp white paper skittered off the table to the floor. "But if you could see the glow, you *are* qualified to be an enforcer. Hmm, let's see, how to explain this to a thirty-year-old rogue?"

"I'm twenty-five," I corrected softly, wondering why I was still standing there, why I hadn't stepped around Kyle and walked out the door.

"You have the ability to see the world differently than this 'real world,' right? Black and white? Plants and animals glow all pretty and clean. People look like they're wearing snowy-weather camouflage. Is this ringing any bells?"

There was definitely a ringing in my ears. He'd just described soul-sight. My knees wobbled and I sank disjointedly into my chair.

Kyle sat across from me, shaking his head with amazement. "I can't believe you've maintained a rogue status for so long. I mean, I understand the appeal of not having a boss, but you're also not on anyone's payroll. Why not become a real enforcer and get paid for it?"

Paid to use soul-sight? Has he infected me with his insanity?

"I, um—"

"Trust me, this region's not hard at all. It's a good place to cut your teeth, but it gets monotonous real fast. Still, let's see what you've got. Tell me what you see here."

"A coffee shop," I said, not quite willing to believe he and I were talking about the same thing.

"Fine. I'll go first." He twitched his long, pointy nose and grinned at me. "You've got great color. Very pure. Which is how I knew you were an enforcer. No *atrum* in sight."

I shifted in my chair, irrationally pulling my suit jacket tighter to cover myself, but Kyle had already turned away.

"Now, that guy behind the counter, he's not the honest type. Look at the way *atrum* coats his fingertips and wrists. Disgusting."

Kyle grinned at me. I tried to remember to breathe. He

was truly talking about soul-sight. I wasn't the only person with the ability. All brain activity got jammed up between that thought and his statement that people—*he*—got paid to use soul-sight. Once I could formulate a complete thought, I was going to have a lot of questions.

"Go ahead, look around in Primordium. I'm going to see if I can attract us a little fun," Kyle said.

For the first time in ten years, I intentionally blinked to soul-sight in public.

I gripped the edges of the table for support against the wave of dizziness that broadsided me whenever I switched between visions; then I purposely examined my surroundings. The coffee shop was slate gray, all color nonexistent in this vision. From the floor (which I knew was tiled white) to the wooden tables to the chrome espresso machine, every inanimate object was shades of charcoal. The overhead lighting didn't exist in soul-sight—*in Primordium,* I corrected myself. Shadows didn't exist in Primordium, either, not traditional light-created shadows. Something worked in this vision to give depth to objects, but trying to focus on it was a recipe for a migraine. The only bright spots in the room were the people.

I forced myself to examine the man behind the cash register to verify Kyle's description, fighting against soul-sight-avoidance instincts honed over the last ten years. My fingers tightened on the table. The barista's fingertips and wrists were smeared black, like he'd had a run-in with a dirty chimney. The rest of his arms were pale gray, as was his face. I knew from experience, those dark patches represented some immoral choices and actions. Light gray was normal for a human; black was pure evil. Only animals and plants were pure white in Primordium. The barista's smudged wrists meant he'd made some bad choices, but I couldn't tell what. That was only one of the flaws of soul-sight.

The only person's soul I'd ever seen that was as pure as an animal's was my own. Since I was far from perfect, I figured I couldn't see my own flaws. That was fine by me. Seeing my soul felt like looking inside myself, and it was a sure way to induce stomach-churning vertigo.

I swiveled my head to look at my companion, fully expecting him to look like a variation of every other human I'd ever seen.

Kyle, the plain-looking salesman, glowed brighter than most searchlights. I lifted my hand to shield my eyes, but it was as impractical as shining a flashlight in my eyes to shield them from the brightness of the sun.

"Aha! There are a few curious imps. Figured there would be with the traffic in here," Kyle said. He was too bright to see his facial features, almost too bright to see a solid outline. When he talked, I couldn't tell if his lips moved. It was one of the creepiest things I'd ever seen.

I had a thousand questions for this man—why had we never met before? Why did he refer to me as a rogue? Could he please dim himself?—but what came out was, "A curious what?"

"Imp." His glowing head swiveled toward me. "You have killed evil creatures before, right?"

I shook my head. "What evil creatures?"

"Amazing. Truly amazing. It's like you've been hiding under a rock, invisible to both sides." He shook his head in wonder. "You've not imploded a single imp? Not even a small one?"

"Maybe I have," I said, belatedly offended and not sure why. "What do they look like?"

Kyle laughed loud enough to draw several stares. "No

shit. A rogue with zero experience." He chuckled again. "The best Brad can attract to his puny region is an untrained nobody with no clue. I'd love to see his face when—" He raised his hand to forestall my next question. "Never mind. You've got the ability; you're trainable. Brad won't turn you away, not when he's so desperate for an IE. Ah, that stands for *illuminant enforcer*, which is the job I'm leaving to you. So let me give you your first demonstration of what a true enforcer does. Watch carefully."

I tore my eyes from his shining aura. There was no after-image like with real light, which was a good thing, because I'd have been blind for a half hour after staring so hard. Logic said the bright light of Kyle should have cast shadows all over the room, but in this strange sight, logic didn't apply.

I wasn't sure where I was supposed to look, so I scanned other customers.

The coffee shop was busy but not full, with groups of two and three people scattered around the free-floating tables—mostly college students or businesspeople escaping the office. People firmly rooted in reality, not looking at dirty souls and talking about illumi-something enforcers and Primordium.

I focused on the group of four people to my right. Like everyone else in the room, they had gray dollops peeking through the V-necks of their shirts and flecks of black soot defiling their hands and wrists. I could see their features faintly through their bodies' natural light, and I flushed with embarrassment when all four turned to stare back at me. I rarely let myself use my soul-sight around people; despite my discomfort, it was heady to use it so blatantly now. Of course, to them it just looked like I was staring rudely.

"Do you see the imps?"

I swiveled back to Kyle and blinked against his brightness. Unobtrusively, I leaned against the table while the world spun back into color.

"They're the smallest of the evil creatures, little blobs of pure evil. Hardly enough brain matter to function. Just enough to recognize food and attack it."

Not good. This is so *not good.* I wished I were back at home with my cat, Mr. Bond, and a good book or a TV show. Something ordinary. I did not want to be talking with the only other known person with soul-sight who kept insisting there were evil creatures visible to only us. I felt like a character in a horror movie right before they slowly turn around and come face-to-face with a monster. Seeing evil on people's souls was bad enough. I didn't want to see—let alone come into contact with—something purely evil.

And yet, how could I *not* look?

I blinked, carefully focusing away from Kyle first.

I scanned the room again. Baristas. Customers. Books and CDs. Coffee bags. "What am I looking for?" Kyle didn't answer me. Movement under the nearest table caught my attention. An inky black chinchilla-like blob sat on the table's base, its glowing eyes watching me.

"What the hell is that?" Anything with life was always a version of white. Even the sullied souls of the sadistic still glowed with light undertones. Nothing living was all black—it was life that made everything glow. Furthermore, animals were never tainted by ambiguous moral choices like humans; animals were *always* white. The tiny fluff ball of blackness was darker than the inanimate objects around it. It was black—solid black. Impossibly black. Either there were varying degrees of life I'd never encountered and this was the zombie equivalent of life, or this creature—this pile of dust with bright eyes—was pure evil.

"Madison, meet your first imps," Kyle said.

The imp cocked its head at me, clearly curious. Curious meant it could think. Curious meant it was trying to puzzle me out. A thinking *evil* creature was interested in me. Abandoning my job hunt and moving back in with my parents suddenly seemed like a great idea.

The imp hopped toward me.

I lurched to my feet, sending my chair careening into the people behind me. Scrambling around the table, I put distance between myself and the creature. Its eyes tracked me. It hopped out from under the table until it was less than two feet away from me. I tensed to flee.

Kyle waved his radiant hand in front of the imp the way a matador waves a cape for a bull. Like a bull, the imp charged. I squealed. The imp disappeared.

He'd said imps, *right? With an* s? I spun around, looking for more.

I spied three behind Kyle's chair. Like the first one, the dark creatures were fixated on him. In a group they lunged. I jumped back, tripping over a chair. Windmilling my arms, I fought for balance while trying to keep the evil creatures in my sight, but gravity won. In a cacophony of wood and metal and flesh, I crashed to the floor. When I looked back at Kyle, the imps were gone.

"Miss? Are you okay?"

Reality popped like my ears had just unplugged. I blinked. The world swam. From my position on the gritty floor, I could see a circle of black-clad feet, and more approaching. Baristas. Everyone in the coffee shop had gone deafeningly quiet, making the cheerful jazz sound like it was blaring. I realized three things simultaneously: (1) *everyone*—from the patrons to the dishwasher—was staring at me; (2) I must look like I had gone absolutely, start-raving mad; and (3) my skirt was hiked up to my hips. *Shit. Can you die from embarrassment? Please?*

I untangled myself from the rungs of the chair I'd tripped over; stood faster than I should have, assisted by the adrenaline of embarrassment; and yanked my skirt down so that it covered me to my knees. I patted at my hair, pulling a bit of muffin out of a clump and wiping my hand on a napkin. And I assured everyone that I was fine, convincing no one.

How could I be fine? I'd just learned that I wasn't the only person with soul-sight—or the ability to see in Primordium. Worse, there were evil creatures that lived alongside us, visible only in Primordium. Creatures that gazed upon me and Kyle with the same loving look I reserved for triple chocolate fudge cake. Somehow Kyle had made them disappear, but for all I could tell, it was magic, because how did you use a sight to make something vanish? I wouldn't have believed it if I hadn't just seen it. It was the equivalent of a person using their normal sight to move an object; it just didn't happen.

Only it had.

ABOUT THE AUTHOR

REBECCA CHASTAIN is the *USA Today* bestselling author of the Madison Fox urban fantasy series and the Gargoyle Guardian Chronicles fantasy trilogy, among other works. Inside her novels, you'll find spellbinding adventures packed with supernatural creatures, thrilling action, heartwarming characters (human and otherwise), and more than a little humor. She lives in Northern California with her wonderful husband and three bossy cats.

Visit RebeccaChastain.com
for updates, extras, and so much more!

Chat with Rebecca on
Facebook: facebook.com/rebeccachastainnovels
Twitter: @Author_Rebecca
Instagram: @chastain.rebecca

FROM *USA TODAY*
BESTSELLING AUTHOR

REBECCA CHASTAIN

Madison's new job would be perfect,
if not for all the creatures trying to
eat her soul...

A FISTFUL OF EVIL
A FISTFUL OF FIRE
A FISTFUL OF FROST

PRAISE FOR THE MADISON FOX NOVELS

"Rebecca Chastain has a hit series here,
one full of humor, danger and amazingly
awesome characters!"
–*Tome Tender*

"a masterfully plotted urban fantasy... I highly
recommend it to readers of all ilk, urban fantasy
aficionados, or not."
–*Open Book Society*

"a great mixture of action, danger, fantasy,
and humor"
–*Books That Hook*

RebeccaChastain.com

– NOW AVAILABLE –

Don't miss a one-of-a-kind hilarious adventure
from *USA Today* bestselling author

Rebecca Chastain

TINY
GLITCHES

Dealing with her electricity-killing curse
makes living in modern-day Los Angeles
complicated for Eva—and that was before
she was blackmailed into hiding a stolen
baby elephant and on the run with Hudson,
a sexy electrical engineer she just met.

"I laughed out loud too many times to count."
—*Pure Textuality*

RebeccaChastain.com

www.ingramcontent.com/pod-product-compliance
Lightning Source LLC
Chambersburg PA
CBHW020618120726
47905CB00003B/846